SYSTEM FAILURE

Book 1 of the Thunderstrike Diaries

Wendy Metcalfe

First published in the United Kingdom 2024 by Wendy Metcalfe

ISBN 978-1-0686506-0-4
Cover design by Getcovers

CHAPTER ONE

I WAS A SPECTACULAR FAILURE as a Predatorbot. Humans had tried to make my fierce female lion self into a heartless killing machine. So far, I've failed to kill dozens of them.

I was created by the Human Collective's Predatorbot Programme, bred in one of their artificial wombs. They implanted me with processors, memories, and behaviour module when I was four months old. They bioengineered me to speak, and they taught me language.

I currently lay on the deck beside the captain's seat in the control room of the Collective Starnavy frigate *Thunderstrike*. *Thunderstrike* had been my home for the last five Standards.

"Stripping the sats now," Strike said. Strike was the sapient machine intelligence who inhabited *Thunderstrike's* systems. He was my best friend in all the universe. "Coms traffic is your regular ag colony minding its own business. I'll run the encrypted messages through my code keys before you drop. We'll make orbit in twenty hours."

Above me, in the captain's seat, Bahar yawned. She was a small, wiry, human woman with night-black skin. She wore faded blue fatigues, and her hair had been released from its braids and formed a curly black halo around her face.

Bahar and I were the only bridge crew Strike had, if you could call me crew. Fugitive, and sometimes argumentative friend, described me better.

"Go get some sleep, you two," Strike said.

He let us out of the control room and I padded into the long hallway. My quarters were the First Officers' suite, through the door on the left next to the control room. The bunk which had taken up most of the space when I arrived was folded into the wall. In its place was my large cat bed. I smoothed out a wrinkle in my blankets with my paw, and settled into it, turning over onto my side, burying my nose into the familiar and comforting scents.

"Sweet dreams, Snap," Strike said.

I didn't have a name before I met Strike. The Predatorbot Programme only gave us numbers. Strike refused to call me by my number. He named me Snap, because my jaws are reinforced and I can snap… you get the idea.

It's another part of the heartless killing machine. They should've removed my heart if that's what they wanted.

When I first came aboard, Strike disabled the kill switch which the Programme had added to my behaviour module. They'd started out adding shock circuits, but you know the jokes about herding cats. The shocks hurt, but we ignored them.

We had no intention of being used as tools by corrupt politicians. The data they'd filled our memories with had changed us. We were no longer simply cats. We were beings who –sort of – understood human culture and politics. We were not going to kill protestors who had legitimate grievances against the Collective.

I'd wanted Strike to remove my behaviour module when I came aboard, but he'd refused. He said it had dozens of connections into my brain, and trying to remove it might kill me. So it still sits in my chest, a malevolent reminder of my origins.

My mentor at the Programme, Nyla Vatan, got me onto *Thunderstrike* shortly after she learned about our kill switches. She later outed the illegal research the Programme was doing, and sensibly went on the run. I haven't heard from her since.

Strike suspected that Collective President Klas Jorrak had ordered the Predatorbot research. He'd been President for fifteen Standards now, and the complaints against him – and the corruption rumours – were steadily growing. Presidential elections came up again in a Standard's time. Stike thought Jorrak planned to use the Predatorbots to dispose of people who threatened his re-election.

Strike had found corruption linked to the President on Arjun and Naretha, and he'd decided he had to act against the man. But Strike was part of the Collective Starnavy, and openly acting against the elected President was technically treason. So he'd had to get sneaky about it.

He founded the Special Investigations Unit. The Collective Starnavy was vast, and there were dozens of offshoot units nobody knew much about, so it was good cover. Strike made sure the Unit looked official, and that we stayed 'under the radar' as he put it.

We are the keepers of the Collective's conscience.

We'd been travelling along the Central Spine route towards the Zurrial Triangle. Strike thought we'd have the best chance of finding Nyla there. But when we docked at Olianna Station our Unit contacts had forwarded files about an illegal mining operation on Reeva.   Someone on the planet had sent a message, hinting at colony charter violations.

Something about it had bothered Strike. He suspected that Jorrak was involved in the mining operation. We'd soon find out whether his suspicions were right.

Eighteen hours later we entered low orbit around Reeva. As we circled the planet a massive open-cut mine came into view. It was in the barren north of the planet's biggest continent, and wasn't destroying any habitat – yet. That wouldn't last if they scaled up production, which our contact here clearly thought they intended to do.

Bahar was wearing one of her Starnavy uniforms this morning, something she only did if she had to look official. We avoided those situations as much as possible.

"Contact with colony initiated," Strike said.

A brown-skinned human's face came up on the wallscreen. Strike added data in a sidebar: Umran Cahul. Colony Chairperson. Male.

"You're on," he told Bahar.

Bahar sat up straight in her seat. "Good morning," she said. "This is the Human Collective frigate *Thunderstrike*. We've received a message from you requesting assistance. Can you clarify what help you need?"

She sounded calm, but her smell had an edge of anxiety to it. That was one of the things the Programme's bioengineering had done to me. I can smell humans' emotions. It wasn't always an advantage.

Umran's face shifted to that expression humans use when they're trying not to react to something. "I didn't ask for assistance. No-one on the Council did. Our colony's functioning just fine." He sounded defensive, and his body had stiffened-up.

I secured a feed line to Bahar and Strike. *Ask him about the mine?* I sent.

Not yet, Strike replied. *We need to figure out what's going on here first.*

Umran was talking again. "We have had some satellite outages recently. Perhaps our engineering chief asked for help with those." Something in the way he said that told me him and the

Chief didn't get on.

"We'll take a look at them. And if you do need help, here are our com codes." Strike sent them, then broke the connection.

"What do you think of that?" Bahar asked.

"I think we worried him. He wasn't expecting a call from us," Strike said.

"That's my reading too," Bahar replied. "Now we have to work out who our real contact is – and what's going on here."

CHAPTER TWO

"RECEIVING NEW CONTACT," Strike said. "It's a shielded line."

The face which appeared on the wallscreen was black-skinned and lined, with long locs streaked with grey. He had the lean look of an ex-trooper.

"Hello, *Thunderstrike*? Are you receiving me?"

"Loud and clear," Bahar said.

"I'm Xannon Naaman. Engineering chief here. An' I'm not happy about what's going on."

In the feed, Strike sent, *The line's secure.*

Xannon smiled. Was that an attempt to charm Bahar? Good luck with that. She described herself as 'sex repulsed aromantic asexual'. She'd had to explain to me what that meant.

"What's the problem?" she asked.

"They're mining. Trashing our world illegally."

"I'm guessing you want us to stop them?"

Xannon's face cycled through a complicated set of emotions. I identified relief, anger, fear, and uncertainty.

"We should talk face to face about this," he said. I saw Bahar hesitate. That was a classic flytrap. "I'm not confident I can keep our coms secure."

That… was interesting. Who didn't he trust here?

"Can you guarantee us safe passage?" Bahar asked.

"Can guarantee you a safe reception."

"So where are you?" she asked.

A set of co-ordinates and a map appeared on the wallscreen. I saved the data to my memories. "This is a remote engineering station. I work out of here now. Left Prairie City when certain people grabbed power," Xannon said.

Right. I've lost count of the number of corrupt governmental structures we've helped to demolish. No, I haven't. The total currently stands at 23.

"Who approved that mine?" Bahar asked.

"Rotten elements on our Council."

That's the tricky kind of intervention. We don't know for certain how many hostiles we've got. And if you think all colonists are idealists wanting a fresh start away from Central, think again. Sometimes they're just criminals looking for a new opportunity.

"When would be the best time to drop?" Bahar asked.

"18.00 local. Going dark here then, and it's changeover for security shifts. Easier to slip past the scanners. Here's my com codes."

"Look out for us then," Bahar replied.

Strike killed the line. "No attempted hacks of our coms. You'll be taking the Xenophon down there."

"Are you suggesting that because you're expecting trouble?" I asked. That shuttle was armed and armoured, and had room for all twenty of our troops. They were currently in cryogenic suspension in Strike's bay.

"You're taking it because it has the best stealthing," Strike said.

"So who's going?" I asked.

"Me," Bahar said. "Five of the troops, and Snap."

I don't think you should go, Strike said over my private feed line.

I need to go to keep Bahar safe.

The troops…

Are obvious targets. I'm not. Nobody here should know what a Predatorbot is. I'm the secret weapon.

Bahar turned to me. "Have you two stopped fighting?" she asked.

"How did you know we were fighting?"

"Because you're glaring at the camera. You only do that when the two of you are disagreeing."

Right. Yeah, that's totally a thing. She says we bicker like an old married couple, whatever that means. The thing is, Strike is very special to me.

Someone else who is very special to me is Nyla. She's an animal neuroscientist. She kept asking awkward questions at the Programme, and got told to shut up. When our kill switches were installed someone leaked the information to her. She quit the

Programme then. She's been laying low ever since, and I really wish I knew where she was.

I panicked when learned about my kill switch. I couldn't block its operation. They had no intention of letting their Predatorbots escape from their slavery. But I did escape, and Nyla was the person who arranged that. I owe her for my freedom. Now I need to find her, and her sisters, and make sure they're all safe. I hope we find some clues to them here.

In the hours before we dropped Strike sent drones down to check the planet out. They did a full orbital sweep of the land. Reeva's feed was pretty quiet, most of the talk about farming or trading. Their security system was tougher to hack, but no match for Strike. And that turned up a curious thing.

You'd think people would object to miners putting a big gash in their planet without their consent, but there was no mention of it. The mine was on the northern side of the mountains, and all the settlements on the southern side of that continent. But even so, I'd expect more noise. Humans complained about everything.

Which meant that most colonists probably didn't know the mine was there. And that the colony's Council was probably involved in the mining operation.

Bahar fretted as usual while Strike thawed the troops out. In between missions they slept in Strike's cryo bay. Strike was a modestly-sized ship, and he only had four decks. The cryo bay was on Deck Three, and took up a large part of the space at the rear of the ship.

Bahar rode down in the lift to Deck Three, and Strike let her into the bay. It was long and narrow, with ten pods on either side of a central accessway. Bahar paced along the rows, checking the readouts of each pod as she passed. It was all totally pointless. Strike ran the show here. He could've told her everything was fine, but this was one of what Strike called 'Bahar's essential rituals'. Humans had lots of those. They really are a weird species.

Strike had chosen Howin to lead the squad, and she strode into the galley an hour before drop. She was tall, broad, and white-skinned, and wore her black hair short in the style of most Starnavy troops. Her scent was completely calm. This was business as usual for her. She flopped into a seat at the galley and said, "Feed me. And brief me."

"Food coming up," Strike said.

I was glad we were taking some of the troops with us. Something about the situation down there didn't feel right.

A shipboard hour later Bahar and I went down to the vehicle bay. The troops had already settled into the shuttle. The lift car let us out on Deck Four, the ship's lowest level. The vehicle bay was the biggest of Strike's three holds here. I padded across the cold deck beside Bahar, and Strike opened the shuttle's airlock door for us. We went to the control room. Bahar took the captain's seat, but Strike would be piloting. The troops were already strapped in in the passenger compartment.

"Sealing up now," Strike announced over the shuttle's com. The vehicle bay doors opened, revealing a square of black outside. "Out you go."

What's the satellite status? I asked over our private feed line as we came into the black.

You're stealthed. Nothing they have up here can register you.

I'd heard that before. Once Strike had been spectacularly wrong about it. I hoped he was right this time.

"Commencing drop now," he said.

We came into atmosphere over the ocean, around the farside of the planet from our destination. "No pings yet," Strike said. "Defence sats coming back on-line now. Still no pings. Not much traffic on this ocean."

Reeva seemed to be the perfect ag colony. I didn't trust that.

We crossed the terminator into the nightside of the planet. Our destination was coming up fast below us. The engineering station was totally dark, and the drones Strike had sent over the area ahead of our drop had recorded minimal power usage.

"Ping from our contact's security system now. ID request received," Strike said. "Let's see what happens. Sending our data."

Why are our weapons hot? I asked over our private feed connection.

Just a friendly warning, Strike replied.

That's not going to get his co-operation.

He asked for our help. Just letting him know what he's dealing with.

Bahar turned to me. "Are you two fighting again?"

"Having a difference of opinion. I don't think we're being very friendly," I said.

Bahar's gaze flicked to the console in front of her, with its weapons status lights. "We'll see," she replied.

I was wearing my armour, but it wasn't sealed up. When it was retracted it covered only my back. I'd set the camouflage to look like a metallic coat for a petbot, complete with a bogus manufacturer's logo. Strike had got the armour for me shortly after I came aboard. Don't ask where it came from.

I don't seal my armour up unless I'm in trouble, and by then it doesn't matter if people find out what I am. I have a weapon on my forehead, and one on each shoulder of my armour. They're operated by my tongue and shoulders, and they stay retracted into my armour most of the time. Most of the time I'm pretending to be a petbot. It works better than weapons for getting information out of people.

Bahar has a saying about us always walking a tightrope. She had to show me images of one to get me to understand. She's right.

The Special Investigations Unit is a large network of humans and machine intelligences. The Collective sprawls over a huge area of space, and you know humans. There are always some who can't resist the lure of a corrupt 'get-rich-quick-scheme', as Bahar calls it. These are the people we find and expose.

If the Starnavy knew about the Unit it would label us traitors. But traitors like overthrowing elected governments. We don't want to do that. We have no desire for power. We just want to see it used fairly and legally.

Lights appeared below the shuttle, outlining a drop pad. The cabin went quiet as the main engines shut off and the antigrav system lowered us onto the pad.

"Just got another ping," Strike said. "Xannon says welcome."

"Let's hope we are," I replied, as I padded to the airlock in front of Bahar and the troops.

CHAPTER THREE

THE AIRLOCK OPENED ONTO A cold night and an absence of weapons fire. That was a good start. I trotted down the ramp and Strike released a dozen drones above us.

The troops clustered around Bahar. They'd perfected the art of looking like a serious threat while appearing as friendly unarmed civilians. Spoiler: they weren't. There's some serious armour and firepower there.

Lights appeared in the lobby of a nearby building. "Why are they operating dark?" Bahar muttered.

"He said he'd left the city. Maybe he doesn't want to be noticed," I replied. At least, I hoped it was that. There was always the chance that this was a sting set up by Central to trap us. It's the tightrope thing again.

Howin led the group over to the lighted lobby. The feed ID of the human standing in the doorway confirmed he was our contact. I sent mine and Bahar's back.

And yes, I do go by the name of Snap. Bahar explains it by saying I snapped at her when we met, and that's why she bought me. She wanted a petbot with a personality.

Don't get me started on that. I can cope with the dumb ones with minimal processing power, but the high-intelligence personal companion bots really bother me. Some are near-sapient, and they're trapped in bodies which humans consider cute or sexy, or… Don't go there, Snap. Focus.

I padded right up to our contact and he didn't step back, but I saw the narrowing of his eyes at my boldness. I was crowding his personal space, testing him. He didn't flinch at all. This looked like one tough ex-trooper. He didn't even smell frightened.

"Snap, where are your manners?" Bahar said. "Stop bothering the man."

"Not bothering me," Xannon said. And really I wasn't. He just thought I was a petbot with weird protocols.

I came to Bahar's side. *Initial survey shows Xannon is armed with a heavy-duty energy pistol*, Strike said over our feed line. *There are energy weapons in the ceiling and walls in the hallway behind him, to take out exterior threats. One's big enough to put a dent in the shuttle's hull. Keeping the shields up.*

"Need to talk in private," Xannon said, eyeing the troops. I caught a spike of uncertainty-scent from him. Good. The troops bothered him.

I'm 95% sure he's genuine, Strike said over our feed. *He hasn't alerted anyone to us.*

"I'd like to bring my petbot," Bahar said. "It acts as my secretary."

Xannon's face cycled through several expressions. I got the idea he didn't believe her, but couldn't think of a good way to say no. He was the one who'd asked for help. He couldn't be fussy about the form it came in.

"Okay," he said, after a brief pause. "We'll go to my office."

Bahar turned to Howin and said, "Wait here."

Howin flicked her a quick hand signal. "Understood." Her scent was mildly anxious, but under control.

Xannon led us down the hall. *Two weapons in the ceiling here*, Strike said, *but they're powered down*. Xannon's office was at the end of the hall, and the heavy door into it was armoured. As it opened Strike sent two of his drones inside ahead of us. The roof was held up by an ironwork lattice. *Scanners on the girder. Going dark now*, Strike said. He settled the drones up by the ceiling.

"Sit down." Xannon offered Bahar a soft couch which was battered but looked clean. She settled there and I took up a position between her and the contact, ready to leap at him if he turned hostile.

"So what do you want us to do here?" Bahar asked. "What do you know about that mine?"

"Not much. Sent a couple of guys to talk to 'em, ask what they were doing. They never came back." I got a burst of anger-scent from him then.

"Did the miners kill them?"

"Suspect so. Thing is, our Charter says no mining. So either those guys ain't read it, or they gone rogue."

What do you think? Bahar asked over our feed line.

I don't think he's lying, Strike replied.

"What about your security system?" Bahar asked. "You have defence sats."

"Yah, we do. Thing is, the ones that should be scanning that region keep going out. We get data for a few days, then they go offline again. Suspect somebody's messing with 'em."

That would have to be a Collective tech, Strike said. *They wouldn't give the codes to planetary security.*

They're the people who need them. Bahar was indignant.

Yeah, she should be. But if you gave colonists the access codes to their sats they'd fix them when they went down. Then you'd lose the option to turn up without warning any time you wanted.

"So what assistance do you need from us?" Bahar asked.

"Was wondering if you'd be willing to go take a look at that mine and ask 'em what the hell they're doing."

Bahar leaned back in her seat. "Let me get this right. You want to send the strangers you called for help into a situation where there's a risk they'll get killed?"

Xannon looked down. His scent changed to embarrassment. Yeah, that's totally what he'd been planning to do.

"We'd need a lot more data about the operation first," she said. "Like the number of personnel at that mine, and what weapons they've got."

"I thought our message would bring a troop carrier," he said. Did I believe that? No, I didn't. His scent told me that was a lie.

"There are too many conflicts going on across Collective space for that," Bahar replied. That wasn't the real reason we were here, but we had no intention of telling him about the Unit.

Anger flashed across his face. "So 'cos we're isolated from Central we're getting abandoned," he snarled.

That was definitely happening to some of the Outlier colonies. The Collective needed to reduce the population in the Central Worlds, so they sent their excess numbers to the Outliers, on the edge of Collective space. They could conveniently forget about them there.

Bahar engaged Xannon with one of her famous stares. They even bother me. "You didn't say in your message that people had been killed. We got the impression this was a minor disagreement."

Before he could answer, an alarm on his desk display blared. "Something's coming into orbit," he said.

Now it gets interesting, Strike said over our feed.

CHAPTER FOUR

"SHIELDED SHIP," XANNON SAID. "Not answering ID hail." Now he smelled worried. That was actually a good sign. It meant this ship entry into the system wasn't pre-planned – or at least, not by him.

Bahar exchanged a look with me. We were probably dealing with a stealthed Collective ship here. Had somebody caught up with us at last? "No offence, but we're leaving," she said. "We'll contact you when it's safe."

"Understood," Xannon replied, and opened the office door. "When you find out what's going on, let me know."

Bahar nodded, but didn't agree to that. What data we passed on depended on what was happening up there. And whether this was about the Unit or not.

As we came into the lobby we picked up the troops. "We're leaving," Bahar said, not checking her stride. The troops fell in behind us.

We're on our way out to the shuttle, I sent to Strike over our feed.

Get aboard fast, Strike ordered.

The door at the end of the hallway was still open, and as we came outside Bahar broke into a run. I cantered beside her, aware of the troops' boots thudding on the plascrete behind us.

My claws clicked on the metal as I climbed the shuttle's ramp behind Bahar. Howin came in last, and as soon as she'd cleared the airlock Strike lifted the shuttle.

"Our visitor is the Starnavy cutter *Redlance*," he said over the shuttle's com. "She only carries a crew of twenty people, so this isn't an invasion."

"So what is it?" I asked.

"That's what we're about to find out."

"We need to move from here," Bahar said. "We're horribly exposed."

"You do," Strike agreed. "I'll move you to the mountains."

The mountains were a long way south-east from this remote engineering station. I knew Strike would've liked to stay here longer. His drones had only explored half the site. The parts they'd got access to held standard power generation and coms facilities, but it was always the parts you couldn't see that held the dangerous stuff.

The shuttle was running dark again. That, along with the stealthing, should stop anyone from tracking us. We were skimming along the edge of the ribbon of trees which joined up with the forest on the northern side of the mountains. This planet was full of trees. Trees held danger. I'm a lion, but I evolved to live on open grassland.

It was 20.00 local time when Strike settled the shuttle into a small clearing close to the far eastern edge of the mountains.

"Is this a natural feature?" Bahar asked, studying the shuttle's night vision images.

"Hard to tell," Strike replied. "But it does make a good surveillance position."

"It does," I agreed. We were hidden behind a thin veil of foliage, but there were enough gaps in it for the shuttle's scanners to get good images of the land beyond the forest.

To our north and east the terrain was flat open grassland. The mine lay north-west of our position, and was hidden from view by the mass of forest trees.

The shuttle's night vision cameras showed the glowing outlines of grazers moving about on the grassland. There were some big herds out there.

I've never hunted live prey. I've always been fed on printer meat substitutes. When I saw open grasslands like this I sometimes wondered what it would feel like to chase prey, to bring it down, apply that killing bite which ended its life.

No, maybe not. Lions don't think about the life they're snuffing out. It's pure survival for them. They're what Bahar calls 'obligate carnivores', and they need to kill to survive. But I've been uplifted. I can think about the loss of life.

Nobody warned us that sapience could be a curse.

"There are some metallic elements in those mountains," Strike said. "They'll help mask you from scans."

That was good. I had a bad feeling about our visitor. And yes, my gut feel is a thing. Bahar says I have good instincts.

Strike shut down the shuttle's drive and sent us data on our visitor. "Only the one ship," he said.

"Not much use as an invasion force," Bahar replied.

"No." I had a really bad feeling about this now. "But it's a perfect size for bringing in miners. Especially if those miners are unwilling recruits."

"Do you think that's what this is?" Bahar asked.

"I've heard rumours of colonists being snatched and used as forced labour." Strike's tone was a mixture of anger and cynicism. Technically, he might be a rogue, but his 'moral compass', as Bahar called it, always pointed true north.

"We need more data," she said.

"I'll send drones out," Strike replied.

He sent them out of the airlock and skimming along the northern boundary of the forest towards the mine. He put their images up on the wallscreen, and the mine's contours appeared.

There was a scatter of prefab buildings on the surface at the edge of the huge open-cast scar. The *Redlance* had landed close to the largest building. The ship's airlock opened, and Strike zoomed the drones in on the figures who stepped out. They were armoured, with faceplates down, but behind them I could see a cluster of people in civilian clothing huddled together.

"Sending the drones in for a closer look," Strike said. "Uh-oh. Alert." The feed disappeared from the wallscreen. "They've spotted the drones. I'm pulling you out of there. Launching now. Strap down." The shuttle lifted off. "I resent having to abandon those drones, but we can't risk whoever's over at the mine tracking them back to you."

The grassland whizzed by beneath us, then the main engines fired. Bahar always wanted to strap me in when we launched, but that had bad associations. It triggered memories from the Programme, and they weren't good.

We climbed fast, and were soon into black sky. 5.2 minutes later alarms blared on the captain's panel. "What is it, Strike?" Bahar asked.

"*Redlance* has launched. Analysis of her trajectory says she's headed your way."

"Can you turn her?" I asked. I meant could he recruit the ship's machine intelligence into the Unit.

"I tried. It's clear where her loyalties lie."

"And now she knows we're here."

"Credit me with some intelligence. She doesn't know *I'm* here," Strike said.

That meant he'd made contact using one of his alias IDs. He usually had at least six active at all times. They came in handy when things got too hot for *Thunderstrike*.

But the *Redlance* still knew that *a* ship was here, and if it came looking for us that would be a problem.

"Alert. *Redlance* is following your trajectory. Going to creative stealthing and active course changes," Strike warned. "Hold on."

The next half hour was rough. Strike changed the shuttle's course several times. On our nav display I could see we were getting close to him. At some stage we'd have to line up for a docking, and that would be the tricky part.

Our active stealthing was good, but this was a Collective ship we were up against. I couldn't help worrying if it had effective countermeasures to our disappearing act.

"Lining you up for dock now," Strike said.

2.4 minutes later something slammed into our rear. The lights went out in the cabin, and the recyclers died.

The engines went off-line, leaving us sitting in the quiet and dark.

And *Redlance* was closing in.

CHAPTER FIVE

ENERGY WEAPON BURSTS FROM the *Redlance* passed above and below our shuttle. "Get your armour sealed," Strike ordered Bahar.

A pulse slammed into our rear, and she yelped. An alarm blared on the panel.

I triggered the seal-up of my armour, lifting one leg at a time for it to close around my paws. My helmet locked and I checked the HUD, putting the atmosphere recycler on line. I'd be good for around thirty hours.

"You okay?" I asked Bahar. Her fear-smell had cut off when I sealed my armour. I accessed her suit's controls and ran the diagnostics.

"I was going to say yes, but I won't bother," she said as she sat down. She sounded annoyed. That was stupid. I was only trying to keep her safe. Didn't she understand that?

The shuttle jerked, and Bahar yelped. New energy bursts passed us. Strike had moved us so that he could fire his wing guns. He had two big wings with six guns on each, mounted at the level of Deck Three. He also had two fins on top of his hull, and they had heavy-duty long-range guns. The *Redlance* was too close to us to use those, but the wing guns were firing continuously.

Thunderstrike's vehicle bay came up ahead, its airlock open.

"Luck," Strike said. "You still have working thrusters. Getting you aboard now." As we came into the bay another energy burst slammed into our rear. The captain's panel erupted with alarms.

"Fire!" Bahar yelled. "They broke through the hull."

"You're home. You're safe," Strike said. "Get into the bay."

Bahar froze for a moment. "Come on," I said.

The sharpness in my voice got through to her. "Yes, of course." She stood up. "Go, Snap."

"Opening airlock," Strike said.

My armour's heating circuits kicked in as I trotted down the ramp into the vehicle bay. I could hear the thud of Bahar's boots behind me. Howin clattered down the ramp behind us. Bahar set foot on the deck and froze, staring out into the deep black through the open bay door.

Howin moved in front of her, blocking her view of the outside, and Bahar relaxed. I had no problem with the idea of vacuum, but the bay was cold, even through my armour's protection. We needed to get out of here soon.

Strike closed the airlock doors and said, "Brace for microjump."

Thunderstrike jumped, and he said, "That's confused *Redlance*. We should be stable for a while now."

The troops had stayed aboard the shuttle to monitor the fire. It had broken through to the pressurised passenger cabin, but the vacuum in the vehicle bay had put it out. Now they appeared in the bay. "All fires extinguished," they confirmed.

"Good. Bay air-up starting now," Strike said.

After 23.6 minutes he let us into the intermediate airlock. Howin led Bahar into the ship and took her up to Deck Three in the lift. Bahar was showing signs of shock. Howin would deal with her trauma. You thought Starnavy captains didn't get traumatised? Think again.

I unsealed my armour and took in the familiar pine scent of Strike's atmosphere. He said it was the scent of the northern redneedle from Lilyan. He used it because it calmed humans. Now it calmed me too.

I rode the lift up to Deck Two and padded down the hall to the control room. Strike let me in, and I settled down in my usual space. "What's our status?" I asked.

"We're hanging out in low orbit behind one of the satellite repair bots. It gives us some cover. Ah, *Redlance* has just fired up. Trajectory's away from us. I think she's going for the jump point. Yeah, she's definitely going for jump."

"Why did they attack us?" I asked.

"Because they didn't want to be discovered. I think they've gone rogue – but not in a good way." Strike was quiet for 3.5 minutes. That worried me. Strike is never quiet for that long.

"What's bothering you?" I asked.

"The shuttle. They got through our shielding. They might have got through my piloting module's walls too."

My heartbeat spiked. What he wasn't saying was that he feared the shuttle was infected with malware. Malware which might leap to his core when he piloted the shuttle again.

"We need to do a full diagnostic on it," I said.

"Yes. But I don't want to do that alone. I need a safety buddy."

"Then invite me into your architecture," I said.

We had this thing where my consciousness and Strike's inhabited the same space. It was something we only did on special occasions – or when things had gone 'pear-shaped' as Bahar put it. Like now. I couldn't force my way into Strike's systems. He'd fry my brain in a heartbeat if I tried that. Besides, he was my friend. Friends didn't invade each other's personal space.

"Sending you the shuttle access pathway now," he said.

I slipped into the pathway and was in the shuttle's systems. Strike's consciousness was vast, but being here was less intimidating. He'd walled the shuttle off from his core. I was restricted to this small subset of his systems. It felt far more cosy.

I sensed Strike's massive consciousness beside mine. Whenever I was in danger of thinking I understood the universe Strike reminded me that I knew nothing. His knowledge was huge, but he always said there was more he didn't know.

What do you want me to do? I asked over our private feed line.

Check environmental and sensor suites. I'll take piloting and navigation.

Starting checks now, I said.

I checked the passenger compartment first. It made sense to attack environmental there if you wanted to kill the shuttle's occupants. I couldn't find anything wrong, or any suspect code.

I sent my results into the feed and moved on to check lifesupport systems in the pilot's compartment. I could sense Strike working alongside me, meticulously taking apart the piloting module's code, examining it, then putting it back together. I concentrated on my tasks, and again I couldn't find any malware or traps.

Coming up clear from me, I reported.

Coming up clear on the other functions too, Strike replied. *I don't think they hit us with anything nasty.*

They didn't have time to prepare anything, I said.

I think I actually believe you, he replied.

I'm going now, I said, and withdrew from his systems. I always felt exhausted after sharing Strike's architecture. The extra stress and worry from the attack made it worse this time. *I have to sleep.*

Strike let me out of the control room, and I stumbled into my quarters. His drones removed my armour, and I shook my pelt. I flopped into my bed and curled up on my side.

Thank you, Snap, Strike said softly as I sank into sleep.

I woke feeling ravenous, and Strike fed me. After I'd endured his usual scolding about being a messy cat he said, "Come to the rec area. I've examined all the sats and I've found something curious." He often delighted in making mysterious statements, but now there was a touch of worry to his mental tone.

I stood up and shook my pelt into order. "Then let me out," I said.

He opened the door for me and I padded down the hall. My nose twitched as I passed the galley. Even with the door closed, a cocktail of stale human food smells hit my nostrils.

I entered the rec area. The walls were lined with padded seats in the Collective's usual wine-red and grey colours. As soon as we formed the Unit Bahar took down the large metal embossed Collective logo which had originally occupied the centre of one long wall. Strike had already disabled the surveillance pickups hidden behind it, and instructed every Unit ship to do the same.

So the rec area is a safe place to talk aboard the ship. Howin and the troops were there when I trotted in, and Bahar followed me. Bahar went to the dispenser and got a hot drink. My nose identified it as coffee. She settled into a seat, and I plonked myself down beside her, out of the way of the troops' boots. I didn't fancy being kicked today.

"So what's so important that you need a meeting?" I asked Strike.

CHAPTER SIX

"While you people have been sleeping I've been busy checking the colony's sats," Strike said. "The defence sats are functioning perfectly – apart from the ones with orbits which take them over the mine. They blank out every time they go over there."

"So Xannon was right about interference," Bahar said.

"Yes," Strike agreed. "The sat records have blanks for thirty minutes every time they're over that location."

"So why doesn't that show up on a diagnostic?" Howin asked.

"I think someone in the colony set that up. I examined some of the repair bots. They're programmed not to fix that fault. It's the only way they could maintain that block," Strike said.

"What about the coms sats?" Bahar asked. "We did get a message after all."

"Somebody got creative with those. There are block codes in every sat," Strike said. "They block outgoing messages with keywords like 'help', 'invasion', 'raiders', or 'miners' in them. The blocks will trigger on the phrase 'habitat destruction' too.

"That's a shitty idea," Howin said. "They don't block regular coms, so the colonists think the satellites are working fine. Right up to the point where they call for help."

"That does explain why the message we received was so ambiguous," Bahar said.

"Xannon must've worked out the sat was blocking stuff. He managed to find a phrase the block code didn't trigger on," I replied. My assessment that Xannon was an ally was now at 98%.

"Every buffer was stuffed with outgoing messages," Strike said. "I downloaded them to my storage and I'm working my way through them."

"So what have you found?" Bahar asked.

"Our Colony Chairperson has been making deals with someone. I'm unsure at this point whether his contacts are a legitimate part of Collective Exploration. He invited them in. It seems like being a self-sufficient ag colony wasn't enough for him."

"What do we know about the man?" I asked.

"Ahead of you there, partner. He was in Collective Admin branch before he signed on for this colony. Logistics. Someone started an investigation against him for theft and bribery. He disappeared before Legal got the evidence they needed to convict. He trashed his records on the way out. Forensics are still trying to reconstruct the databases."

"So he's a greedy small-time criminal," Howin said.

"It's looking like it. I've started an investigation into his Colony Leader election here."

"Which may be fraudulent?" Bahar asked.

"You got it. It's not absolutely clear he's behind the mining setup, but I suspect so. I think he's trying to downplay the impact the operation will have on the colony," Strike said.

"Someone should show the colonists images of Triveni," I replied. That whole planet had been mined. It was rich in all the rare stuff the Collective desperately needed. So they stripped it all and killed most of the species which lived there.

I'm touchy about habitat destruction. My species managed to survive because the Central Worlds designated enough reserves in time. They translocated breeding populations of lions to twenty worlds in the Outliers, so our numbers are stable now. And my relatives are a long way from Central's murderous biotech research projects. They should survive. Other species haven't fared so well.

"So do we need to get involved?" Bahar asked.

"I think we need to talk to Xannon again before we make a final decision," I said.

"Agreed," Strike replied. "And… he's calling us now."

Xannon's face appeared on the big wallscreen, and he looked worried. "Glad I got yer," he said. "Just received a message from someone over at the mine. Says she's one of the people they just dumped there. Sending it over to you now."

A female face appeared on the wallscreen, and I froze. Bahar swore.

Oh, yeah. We were totally going to get involved in this. This changed everything.

CHAPTER SEVEN

THE FACE ON THE wallscreen was a young white-skinned woman's. Her image had been stored in my permanent memory since the first time I met her.

She was Fia Vatan, and she was one of Nyla's four sisters. She was the person we'd set out to find on this mission.

"To anyone who receives this message, please help us. We're colonists of Davion. Twelve of us were snatched by the Collective cutter *Redlance*. It's gone rogue. The ship landed at night on our colony and snatched us out of our beds. They're forcing us to work in the mine here."

"Slavery," Bahar snarled.

"Please, help us," Fia repeated.

Shouting started up somewhere behind her, then the sound of heavy footsteps approaching filled the audio feed. The image fizzled out, then the audio blanked.

Xannon was still on the line, and while Bahar talked to him about Fia I had an emotional meltdown. One of Nyla's sisters was in danger. I had to help her.

When I escaped from the Programme, Nyla was the one who got me out of there. She hustled me aboard *Thunderstrike*, risking her own life. I owe my freedom to Nyla. So the least I can do to repay her is to rescue her sister.

Bahar ended her conversation with Xannon and turned to me. "We've got to get her out," I said. She nodded. She didn't ask me who I meant. She knew.

"We do," Strike agreed. "Gotta break up this chain gang."

What had I missed? I re-ran Bahar's conversation with Xannon. Oh, right.

This wasn't the first batch of slaves *Redlance* had dumped at this mine. Xannon had witnessed a previous drop. That was two months ago. So they were scaling up their operation – or the first lot of slaves were dead.

We had to close this mine down. We'd do that even if Fia wasn't here. But now I knew she was, there was no way I was leaving this planet without her.

"Really could use some help to close that mine down," Xannon was saying when I returned my attention to the live conversation.

"Oh, don't worry," Bahar said. "We're not leaving until we've rescued all the slaves."

"Slaves?" The word startled him.

"What else would you call people being snatched out of their beds and being forced to work against their will?"

"That's… yeah, you're right. What help do you need from me?"

"Local intel," Bahar said. She pointed to Howin. "This is Howin. One of our squad leaders. The other one is Rance. They'll be leading the retrieval operation. I'll call you again when they're ready to drop."

"Understood. And thanks for your help."

When Xannon had gone Howin said, "We need the whole squad."

"I've already started wake-up," Strike replied.

As usual, Bahar did her regular inspections of the cryo bay as Strike woke up the rest of the troops. Howin seemed to be strangely affected by it. It had taken me a long time to work out that this was a way Bahar showed her love for people.

She said humans often used the word love when they really meant sexual lust. She said love's real meaning was much wider and meant far more than cheap sex.

Strike spent the hours while we waited for the rest of the troops to wake up repairing the Xenophon. Luckily, the damage to the hull had missed the main engines. But it had hit a set of thrusters instead. Strike carried a whole bank of printers distributed around his shipbody, and he set them to work printing replacements for the slagged parts. He sent his repair bots to fix the hull and put in replacement wiring and sensors.

When he was done, he insisted on running the system check data past me, and sent me to smell the hull repair. The weird thing is, I can smell when a hull feels right. Or rather, I can smell any weak spots in it. This is going to sound weird to you, but to me, a sound hull smells sweet. Any weak spots smell sour. Strike has tried to programme his drones to replicate my smell-sense, but they aren't as accurate as me.

I was glad to have something useful to occupy my time, and went over every inch of the Xenophon's hull. Strike got me onto one of his lift platforms to check the top of the shuttle. I don't like those things, and I was glad when the job was done and I could plant my paws back on the deck.

I couldn't smell any weaknesses, and Strike's system checks had come up clear. We were ready to go when the troops were.

While the wake-up process continued Strike and I studied data for the mine. He'd chosen not to orbit directly above it, in case that tripped alarms on the surface. So our data was coming from the drones he'd sent down.

We'd thought the mine was purely open-cast, but the video on Fia's message had showed she was in a tunnel somewhere. So there must be underground workings too. If Fia was down at deep level, retrieving her alive was going to be a lot more difficult. And we couldn't be certain the data our drones were sending back showed everything down there.

"The troops need to take emergency breathers with them," I said.

"Agreed," Strike replied, and added it to the mission briefing.

That cut down on one danger. At least if we got the people out they wouldn't die of asphyxiation.

The mine had two levels, and we guessed the deeper one was the active mine face. The level above showed a series of square voids. They were probably offices or storage spaces. One very large rectangular void Strike thought was most likely some kind of processing facility.

The open pit was sunk into grey rock. The rock ran right up to the northern coast; one big, barren, grey pavement. We wouldn't be approaching from that direction. The drones' scans revealed that the facility wasn't shielded. They obviously didn't expect anyone to come and attack them. That kind of arrogance is always useful.

The facility had a deep level, and the thing about deep levels is that they're hot. Working down there produces a lot of heat you need to get rid of. Granted, these rogues were slavers, and probably couldn't give a damn if their slaves survived. But heat affected machinery too, and they did care about breakdowns.

So there'd be vents to the surface somewhere, and they were a possible entry point to the mine. It's surprising how many supposedly secure bunkers I've entered through an insecure heat vent.

We were planning to gain entry that way. We needed to find a way in where we wouldn't be noticed. Then we had to find Fia. Chances were they'd put her to work in the mine straight away. Slavers were mean like that. If she was down in the deep level we'd need luck as well as good planning to get her out.

We'd have to make a lot of assumptions in our plans. They wouldn't work as intended.

They never did.

5.6 hours later Strike summoned us all to the rec area for a briefing. The room was large, but with all twenty troops in there it was crowded. That's why they spent most of their time in cryo. It was the most efficient use of our resources.

They were split into two squads. Howin led one, Rance the other. Rance was short, with a brown complexion and curly brown hair cropped short. Howin's gestures were languid and relaxed. Rance was always moving, his eyes darting around the room, his hands constantly in motion. They were opposites. And they bickered, just like me and Strike.

"These damned wake-up drinks never get any better," Rance grumbled.

"Quit bitching," Howin said. "So what are we dealing with this time?"

"The mine's fairly new," Strike replied. He put up a schematic on the big wallscreen, showing the mine's two levels. "Our contact said the first batch of – let's call them miners – were dropped there two months ago. He thinks there were about a dozen. And they dropped a dozen this time too. So we might have a total of twenty-four people to retrieve."

"Going to be crowded on the shuttle on the way back," Rance said.

"Which is why I've aired-up its vehicle bay, and cleared it out. You can ride up in it. The downside is I've had to take out the skimmers. Now here's the serious bit."

Strike played Fia's message for the troops, and I froze again. Bahar was sitting next to me, and she reached down a hand and touched my neck. The warmth of the contact reassured me.

"So this is one of Nyla's sisters?" Howin asked.

She looked at me, but I couldn't meet her gaze. Get your act together, Snap. You're supposed to be a deadly Predatorbot.

"Yes, she is," Bahar replied. "That's Fia."

"Understood."

I understood too. Bahar was serving notice that we weren't abandoning anyone this time.

We were retrieving Fia.

Whatever the cost.

CHAPTER EIGHT

THE NEXT HOUR WAS the usual flurry of pre-mission prep. Bahar would be staying aboard Strike. I had insisted on going down to Reeva with the troops.

Finally we were all settled in the shuttle and strapped-in for the drop. "Taking local defence sats off-line now," Strike said. "Opening bay doors. And here we go."

I felt the jolt as the shuttle's thrusters fired. I was sitting beside Howin, and I was strapped in this time. Howin had insisted on it. I didn't like it, but I'd come to realise that this was the way Howin showed she cared for me.

"Xannon's expecting you," Strike said. "Dropping now."

We dived into darkness, coming into the planet's atmosphere over the southern polar region and losing height over the vast southern ocean. Again, the shuttle's scans showed little moving there. This did seem to be a self-sufficient ag colony. It should do quite well – once the irritation of its greedy Colony Chairperson had been removed.

That was a 'mop-up action' as Bahar called it. I needed to focus on today's task, and I felt tense. That was irritating, but it was a familiar irritation. The idiots in the Programme thought they'd produce fearless killing machines. The Predatorbots they ended up with are pretty much the opposite. We get just as afraid of being killed as humans do.

"Land's coming up," Strike said over the shuttle's com.

There wasn't much to see. The only big light source on the continent was the capital, Prairie City. There were small scatters of light showing at coastal settlements, but the middle of the continent was dark.

That included the mine. There were no surface lights there at all. To me, that marked it out as a suspect operation. If it was a corporate outfit it would've had its logo plastered everywhere. And it would've been expensively and wastefully lit.

Strike turned the shuttle north-west and we came up the western coast of the continent. The settlements of Gafra and Autra showed lights down by their harbours, but the engineering station was completely dark.

We planned to approach it from the ocean. Strike's drones' scans of the exterior of the site had showed that Xannon's defences all faced inland. An ocean approach shouldn't alert him before we arrived.

We waited until we were right on top of the engineering station before we hailed the contact. Xannon answered immediately. The troops were wearing their armour. They looked like a Collective strike squad, but their armour was minus the logos.

"Can we come down and talk?" Howin asked.

The hesitation was three seconds, not long enough for the

humans to notice, but I did. "Sure," he said. "Yah wanna drop yer shuttle on our pad?"

"Will do," Howin said, and cut the contact.

"That scared him," Rance said. "Now he knows not to fuck with us."

I didn't think Xannon would do that anyway, but intimidating civilians often had useful benefits.

Strike put the shuttle down dead centre of the pad. "Thanks, Strike," Howin said. "We'll keep you updated."

"You get those beacons on now," Strike insisted. His voice through the shuttle's nodes was forceful. I switched my beacon live.

"Receiving you all," Strike said. "Off you go, and…"

"Be careful," Howin finished. "Yeah, yeah."

I'm always careful, I said over my private feed connection to Strike.

If that's being careful, then I don't want to be around when you're reckless, he replied.

The shuttle's ramp dropped and the team leaders walked out onto the pad. They had the partial map of the facility which Strike's drones had got on our first visit here stored in their implants. They knew where all the exits on the upper level were. I didn't think they'd need the data, but what was that old motto? Be prepared.

I stayed on the shuttle. Strike had sent two groups of his drones out with the troops, so I'd be able to see and hear what was going on in there. It would save any awkward questions about why the cute petbot was going on this mission. And maybe Strike would get the chance to map more of the facility while they were talking.

Xannon met the troops in the outer hallway. His body was at attention, and I figured he was trying hard not to salute. Yeah, he was definitely ex-military. And yeah, old habits do die hard.

"Welcome to the Engineering Station," he said. "Let's go talk."

He led the troops into a briefing room. Strike settled his drones up by the roof, then knocked the scanners out. They didn't alarm on loss of signal. So Xannon was fairly relaxed about security here. That surprised me. Was it arrogance, or incompetence?

I switched my attention back to the conversation in the room as Xannon asked the team leaders how they'd heard about the mine. This bit was always tricky.

"I don't know who tipped the Starnavy off about the mine," Howin said, "but we were sent to investigate. We've recently investigated a series of abuses of colony charters among the Outliers, and shut down several dangerous operations." That much was true, but we'd done it independently and exposed the Collective's bad actors. "We don't know what they're doing in that mine, but it might be more than ore extraction."

"Whadda yer mean?" Xannon was all attention now. Focusing

on the suspect operation worked as well as it usually did to divert attention away from us.

"There's a bunch called Outlier Action operating in the Zurrial Triangle," Rance said. "They're building up support on many Outlier planets. We think it's the first stage of an operation to split the Outliers off from the Collective. Under their control, of course. This mine might be connected to them."

The organisation existed, but as far as we knew it was a harmless pressure group. We used this script to assess the degree of loyalty of contacts to the Collective.

"Sometimes seems like the Collective's abandoned us," Xannon said. "But I'm not wanting to join some rebel outfit. Might be some in Prairie City who would, though."

"Care to name names?" Howin asked.

"Strictly off the record?"

"Your anonymity is guaranteed," she confirmed. It was a bogus guarantee. Strike's drones were busily recording this conversation.

"You might check into our Chairperson's dealings, but I didn't tell you that," Xannon said.

"Understood. We need to plan our approach and entry to the mine. I'm looking for your recommendations."

The troops returned to the shuttle half an hour later. Xannon didn't have any useful information about the mine itself. He'd never been there.

We left the engineering station and Strike turned the shuttle east. We flew along the northern side of the ribbon of trees which linked this promontory to the main forest. We were flying dark. When we met the first river we turned north and flew up the western coast, over a second river, and past the first trees. Xannon had told Howin there was a broad corridor through them large enough for the shuttle. It would take us right up to the mine.

I didn't trust convenient corridors on unspoiled worlds. It always meant somebody had made them. And the only people who'd need a path through the trees were the people running that mine. So I expected us to trip some alarms going that way. Surprisingly, we didn't. Or at least, our scans didn't pick up any.

While we made our way out to the mine Strike reported on his review of the coms sats' logs. He told us that Umran had regular personal contact with two Collective ships, the *Nebulafire* and the *Starlance*. Something suspect was definitely going on here.

"Nearing the end of the forest," Howin said. "Where's our landing spot?"

"Here," Strike said, and set us down.

The wallscreen lit with a night vision view of the terrain outside, relayed from the shuttle's scanners. We were hidden from the mine by the trees in front of us, but they were thinner here, and there were several broad routes through the boles to the mine boundary. The shuttle could force its way through there if necessary.

"I'm sending my drones out now," Strike said, and opened the airlock to let them go. He sent them over the approach route to our target vent, and also mapped out the routes to the next two nearest ones.

I hadn't realised from the high-altitude scans that the dots on the surface were spoil heaps. Obviously somebody got detailed to dump the spoil at the surface. We thought some of the captives might be put to work in the processing plant, so most likely we'd have to split the squad into two. This happens regularly, and it's why we have two team leaders.

The drones still couldn't pick up any scans. I guess whoever operated this mine wasn't planning on someone hostile entering their facility. Was that arrogance, or incompetence? It made a difference to the way they fought.

There was one small area of open flat ground right in front of Vent One. That could trap us there if the vent turned out to be locked. We couldn't afford to be backed up against the building if things turned bad. It was time to deploy one of the shuttle's maintenance drones to fix that.

Strike let the drone out of the airlock and it whizzed across to the vent. The drone was programmed for opening hatches and wrestling its way into malfunctioning systems. They were the perfect skills for this job.

It was another reason why we had to look like a legitimate part of the Starnavy. Strike received all the new equipment and system downloads. This drone had received the latest updates yesterday. He didn't expect a problem with it getting into the mine.

The drone reported an absence of exterior scans. That wasn't enough to convince me that this would be an easy mission. Things might be very different on the inside.

"Vent's unlocked," Strike said. "They were using a Standard-old code sequence. You can get in there at your leisure."

That meant get moving before somebody noticed his hack. It was time to seal up my armour. Strike's drones had fastened it around my belly before we left *Thunderstrike*. I'd worn it in its usual configuration, with the legs and tail sections, and my helmet, retracted. I didn't seal it up until I really needed it.

I extended the leg sections, lifting one foot at a time to let the armour seal around each paw. I lost a lot of data about the terrain with my paws covered, but it saved them being fried. My helmet extended and locked, and the HUD in its visor fired up. I put my weapons through their self-tests and switched them to standby.

Howin led the way down the shuttle's ramp, into the darkness. Strike's drones formed an advance scan group. They'd warn us if anything tried to attack. My armour registered the temperature out here as around freezing. That might be a problem if Fia's people weren't adequately dressed.

Nothing attacked us when we left the shuttle, and Strike closed up the ramp behind us. That was standard practice, but my anxiety spiked. It always did.

We threaded our way through the trees and halted at their edge. My helmet filters showed up the spoil heaps clearly. My night vision is naturally good, but the armour makes it even better.

"Suit coms on," Howin ordered.

"Receiving," I replied. The troops behind us reported in. I could hear the tension in some of their voices.

We darted between the spoil heaps, making for Vent One. Strike's drones spread out ahead of us. This was too easy. They must have surveillance here.

We weren't exactly sure how many people worked in this facility. We'd picked up around fifty heat sources, but they were always moving, and Strike wasn't sure he had an accurate head count.

We reached the vent and Strike sent the code sequence to unlock the grille. Howin pushed at it. It didn't move.

You said you'd opened this, I sent to Strike over our secured feed line.

I did. Give me a moment. They've just changed the code. Try again.

Howin pushed at the grille again. This time, it swung inwards and she led us into the vent. When we were all inside someone closed the grille behind us. My anxiety spiked again. Yeah, they needed to do that to prevent an alarm firing off, but now we were locked in here.

The drones zipped off down the passageway, sending their images to our feed. The passage sloped steadily downwards. It was big enough for the tallest trooper to walk down without bending their head, and wide enough to take two people side by side. I guessed it had been an equipment access when they were building the facility. There was no light in the passageway, so we needed our night vision filters. The drones were showing us only empty space ahead.

"Let's get down there," Howin said over the feed. She slipped her pistol from its holster and turned it on. I put my weapons on standby.

The passage opened-out into a level hallway. Strike sent the drones into it, and Howin swore. Images came over the feed. There were several humps on the floor.

We were looking at a pile of dead bodies.

CHAPTER NINE

I FROZE. WHAT IF this was… Rance and Howin pushed past me and went to examine the huddled forms. The nearest one had fallen with its jacket over its head, hiding the face. When Howin pulled it back I snarled.

There was only the skull left. She and Rance moved to the other forms and examined them. They were all only bones now. They weren't our current crop of captives.

"They've been here some time," Howin said. "My guess is they were trying to escape."

I didn't answer. I was feeling weak and wobbly as relief flooded my body. These people couldn't be Fia. That was the downside of caring for people. You could feel fear for their safety.

"We need to go on," Howin said. "We'll clear the bottom level first."

I forced myself to walk down the hall. It ended at a lift shaft. The cage was on the surface, and I estimated it would hold fifty people. Winding around the shaft was a circular metal stairway.

"What do you think?" Howin asked.

"They'd notice us using the lift. Reserve it for the way out," Rance replied.

She nodded. "Thought you'd say that. Down the stairs it is, then."

We engaged our softsoles, and went down the metal staircase silently. Strike sent the drones ahead of us. They told us there was no surveillance in the shaft. They hadn't even installed gas monitors there.

This was beginning to look like an amateur operation, and that spiked my anxiety again. Amateurs killed people accidentally. I didn't want Fia dying here.

Strike said I hero-worshipped Nyla. Maybe he was right. She was the only person I'd walk through certain death to rescue, and I didn't want her to lose her sister. This retrieval mattered.

We reached the first level, and Strike sent the drones on ahead again. As we went down to the second level their audio registered noise somewhere below us. It resolved into someone shouting. Strike boosted the drones' audio, but I couldn't make out the words. They were too far away.

The drones were showing us a rough-hewn shaft at the bottom of the staircase. A conveyor ran along the right hand side of it. It looked like we were approaching the working face.

The drones reached the source of the noise. It was some way down the gallery. The shouting came from a huge white-skinned guy. Five people clustered behind him. Their clothes looked rumpled as if they'd been roughly handled. Before I could ask Strike, he zoomed the drones' cameras in on their faces. Fia wasn't with them. A surge of relief and disappointment whipped through my body.

I was right about this being the working face. A huge machine filled the tunnel behind the clustered figures. The teeth in its circular cutting head were exposed, and they looked very worn. Yeah, this was definitely an amateur outfit.

The big guy was facing up to two thugs, telling them the captives weren't going to work for them. That was brave, but risky.

"Two targets," Strike said, and sent the drone video to us. Howin and Rance took off down the hallway.

The noise would alert whoever was running this place, but the hostiles had just pulled out weapons. They were threatening to shoot the captives, and we didn't have time for a stealth approach.

Fia not being here was a relief, but it meant that this operation just got more complicated. Why am I not surprised?

The hostiles had their backs to us and were telling the captives they either worked or got killed. We definitely needed to intervene here. Howin and Rance took the two thugs out.

Some of the captives started screaming, and we didn't need that. Howin raised her free hand in a 'peace' gesture and they actually shut up. It probably helped that she was pointing her weapon at the floor. "We're here to rescue you," she said through her armour's external speakers. "Follow us and we'll get you out of here."

Strike sent his drones ahead of us, and led the ragged band along the gallery. There were still no alarms. I was disappointed that I hadn't found Fia, and my anxiety spiked again.

I had to find her. If they hadn't dragged her down here to do the dangerous mining, where would she be? She'd be doing whatever other work they wanted slaves for. Most likely that meant dealing with the ore the first group mined. Most mines used bots to do that, and it suggested this was a low-resource outfit.

Whoever these people were, they weren't going to make these captives into slaves. And they sure weren't going to do that to Fia.

We reached the lobby, and Howin asked the captives where the rest of their group was. "Ore processing, next level up," the big guy said. "There are six of us there."

We needed to move from here before more hostiles showed up. If we went in the lift it would make noise. But it was the quickest way out, and the captives didn't look like they could handle a hard climb up those stairs.

We need to split the squad, Howin said over our feed. *Rance, you take this group up and make for Vent One. Backup's Vent Two if that's blocked. Get them straight out and onto the shuttle. Don't wait for us. We'll ride up with you to the upper level. If we're drawing attention to ourselves, we might as well use the lift too. I'm assuming the processing facility is the big rectangular void up there.*

That's my best guess, Strike replied.

We got everybody into the lift. The keypad inside the cage required a code. I accessed it and found the code, killing the report function at the same time. We really didn't want that notification telling our hostiles where we were.

The lift stopped on the first level with a clang which echoed up and down the shaft. So much for a stealth retrieval. *We're making a lot of noise,* I sent to Strike over our feed line. *We'll need the shuttle close when we exit.*

I'll set it down by Vent One.

We stepped out of the lift, and the door closed behind us. Strike sent the cage the command to rise to surface level and open its door. I had a moment of anxiety. Would our hostiles try to lock our people into the cage?

Trying to lock us out, Strike said over the feed, confirming my guess. *Overriding.*

I kept my attention on the feed from the drone he'd left in the lift car until the car reached the surface. Its doors didn't open. Someone was giving it the command to descend again. *This is getting tedious,* Strike said.

He told the cage to open its door, and thankfully, it did. Rance ushered the captives out. Strike sent his drones on ahead into the vent accessway, checking for surveillance there. There wasn't any. Rance's group should make it out safely now.

I returned my attention to the feeds from the drones on the first level. The room where I thought the conveyor was had a door which had once been part of a ship's airlock. It might be armoured, and that could give us a problem if we needed to blast a hole in it.

The hallway was clad with rusting metal panels which looked like they'd been salvaged from a derelict ship. There were scans here, and the drones knocked them out. Strike had written some code for them, which took things off-line creatively. It fuzzed the picture before blanking it, and chopped up the audio into meaningless noise. It was supposed to make the takedown look like a system failure and not an attack by hostiles. He hadn't used it before. We didn't know if it would work.

"Scanners are down," he said.

We followed the drones along the hallway to the room where we thought the conveyor was. Strike boosted the drones' audio inputs, and they brought us the sound of voices beyond the door.

Accessing the keypad now, Strike said. The door didn't open. *I've a hunch about where that door came from. Accessing my database of codes from Collective ships. Got it*, he said as the door lock clunked.

The door cracked open, and Strike sent his drones inside. Their video showed us that the rest of the captives were here. *Fia's here*, Strike said, and zoomed one of the drones in on her face. Relief made my body go weak when I saw she was alive and seemed unharmed.

A broad conveyor belt ran across the centre of the room, at my head height. A chute and hopper in the left-hand wall were where the ore was dumped onto the belt. The belt ran on a metal toothed track, and looked like it should be in a history vid. Several teeth showed a lot of wear. The surface of the belt was scratched, and its edges were fraying. This was definitely a low-resource outfit. I didn't rate the safety of that thing.

As we walked inside the room the airlock door auto-closed behind us. That was worrying.

The six captives were on the other side of the conveyor. Three rough-clad men with long untidy hair were showing them how the machine worked.

A tall black man stepped to the front of the group of captives. "What kinda jokers are ye?" he snarled. "Think ye can snatch us outta our beds and make us into slaves? Ye can…"

The hostiles drew their weapons. "You work, or you die," one of them snarled.

Howin turned her external suit speakers up full. "No, you die," she boomed. The hostile swung round to face her, and she shot him in the chest.

The captives ducked beneath the conveyor. The second hostile pointed his weapon down at them. "No you don't you bastard," Howin growled, and shot him.

The third hostile made a lunge for the conveyor's control panel, and set the belt into motion. Then he fired into the panel, frying its controls.

"What the hell?" Howin growled, and shot him.

"Everybody okay?" she called to the captives. "We're here to rescue you."

The captives scrambled to their feet as Strike said in our feed, *Problem. I can't get the airlock door to open. You'll have to go out the other side of the room.*

In the wall opposite, the small personnel door slid open. Strike sent two of his drones out into the hallway beyond.

Juddering and clunking sounds came from the conveyor. The belt was speeding up and slowing down as the toothed bed ground around its circuit. Something was messed up in there, and the thing was struggling.

Howin moved to the control panel and jabbed the off switch. The belt kept running. "He fried the controls. Thought so. Let's get outta here," she said.

She hustled the captives away from the conveyor. "We're going out this door," she said, pointing to the small personnel one. "Need to get outta here before that thing shakes itself apart. Move." Her sharp command got the captives on their feet.

We edged around the end of the clattering machine, and the troops surrounded the captives. *Alert from hallway drones*, Strike said in our feed. *Three hostiles coming towards you from the side passage.* Video appeared in my HUD of three armoured figures running towards us. Then my attention went to the figure behind them, and for a nanosecond I froze.

It was a Predatorbot, with its armour deployed.

I was going to have to fight my own kind.

CHAPTER TEN

WHILE I PROCESSED THE appearance of the Predatorbot the hostiles ran in, firing. The troopers returned fire, and the first hostile went down.

I kept my attention on the Predatorbot. What if I could turn it? Offer it release from its behaviour module? I found its coms channel and sent, "Hello, teammate. Would you like to be freed from your behaviour module?"

It didn't have the effect I expected. The cat fired its headweapon at me, and I was forced to return fire.

The noise in the room behind me was getting louder. I could hear the conveyor's belt screeching as it speeded up and slowed down. I turned my armour's sound receptors down, but I couldn't dial down my anxiety. The conveyor would shake itself apart soon, and we had to get Fia out of here before she got hurt. Over the sound of weapons fire I heard the shriek of an alarm. The clattering from the belt was getting worse.

The second hostile went down. The third pulled a box from his pocket as Howin shot him. I sensed the pulse he sent from it a nanosecond too late. The Predatorbot convulsed, then collapsed. I accessed its behaviour module, but I was too late. Catastrophic damage to the brain had already occurred. The cat was dying. I withdrew from the module as the cat's last spark of awareness winked out.

"Snap, get moving!" Howin's voice was sharp.

My limbs felt weak, my body listless. The death of the Predatorbot had left me feeling numb. I'd failed to save it. Another of my kind was dead.

The clattering from the conveyor stopped. Another screeching alarm started up. I turned my head and saw the tattered belt rip itself apart. It leapt off the bed, and I lowered my head fast as it flew towards me. It sailed over me, and slammed into the side wall with a sound like a gunshot.

Something bright flared in my peripheral vision. I turned my head and saw the control panel had flared into flame. I had to get out of here. The control panel's metal casing burst apart, and a large piece slammed into my rump. I snarled. That hurt.

The belt bed decided to join the party. The teeth weren't connected any more, so instead of turning around and going back underneath, they slammed into the wall. Some fell down to the floor, but some had enough velocity to rebound into the room. I ducked my head again as one sailed past me, and picked up my pace. Metal pieces shot into the air all around me. I cantered towards the door.

Another metal tooth slammed into my back. It really hurt, and I snarled again.

"Snap, come on!" Howin's voice was loud and sharp in my suit coms.

The troopers had got the captives out into the hallway. The space in front of the doorway was clear and I took off at a gallop. I barrelled through the doorway and overshot the hall, travelling half way down the side passage before I could stop.

"Fire in there," I told Howin. "We need to move." My anxiety kicked in again. We'd have to take a different lift to the surface, exit by a different vent.

This batch of captives didn't look as roughly-handled as the group from the lower level. Fia looked fine. Howin hustled them along the hallway at a run.

Strike's drones took off towards the lobby, and we followed them. *Lobby's empty*, Strike confirmed over our feed. *Opening the cage door for you now.*

By the time we reached the lift the cage door was open. We stumbled into it and Howin closed the door and jabbed the 'up' button on the panel. Nobody tried to stop us, and we reached the surface 3.3 minutes later.

We waited in the lobby while Strike sent his drones out to Vent Three. *Problem*, he said over the feed. *Not good. There are twelve armed hostiles outside that vent. Go for Vent Four. I'll stage a diversion at Vent Three.*

Agreed, Howin replied, and hustled us past Vent Three's access tunnel. Strike's drones began firing through the grille as soon as we'd passed.

An image from an exterior drone popped up in our feed. The hostiles were fully engaged in trying to slag the drone.

It seemed to take the humans for ever to reach Vent Four, but in reality it was only 6.1 minutes. Strike sent three drones up that shaft and out of the grille. His diversion was working. The hostiles were still firing into Vent Three. Vent Four was clear. But as soon as we exited they'd turn their attention to us.

Setting the shuttle down outside Vent Four now, Strike said in our feed.

Howin entered the code sequence to unlock the grille into the keypad. Nothing happened.

"We don't have time for this," she said. "Get back." She melted the lock with her weapon.

As she swung the grille open I sent, *Strike, where are you?*

Here. Strike's voice was smug. *Shuttle's down. Ramp extending now*, he said as the ramp appeared out of nowhere.

Strike's shuttles were real goodies. As well as being armed and armoured, they were also stealthed. He'd requisitioned an upgrade to that stealthing a Standard ago, and got it. The shuttle was now stealthed in discrete zones, and the only part he needed to take down to let us in was a small square over the airlock.

Howin stepped up to the threshold of the vent, then turned to the captives. "We're going to run to the ramp and go straight up it," she instructed them.

Strike told his drones in Vent Three to up their fire rate. They'd taken out six hostiles, but there were still six remaining.

The squad bunched up around the captives, and they pounded over the rough ground towards the shuttle. Fia stumbled, and one of the troops grabbed her arm and hustled her up the ramp. I was at the back of the group, and as the last of them entered the airlock Howin turned around and said, "Snap, come on!"

I galloped up the ramp, but now the hostiles had realised we'd tricked them, and they turned their fire on me. My armour took a couple of hits. I barrelled into the airlock and dug my claws into the rough matting Strike had deployed there to slow me down. He'd added that after I'd slammed into the inner airlock door head-first on one of our early missions and given myself concussion.

This time, the inner door was open, but I stopped before I reached it anyway. Then I turned around and walked to the open outer door, standing on the threshold while Strike retracted the ramp and lifted off.

The hostiles fired at the shuttle. I tongued my head weapon on and shot at them before we rose out of range.

That was unnecessary, Strike said.

They killed a Predatorbot. Triggered its kill switch.

Oh. Strike shut up.

I walked through to the passenger compartment and Strike

closed the door behind me. *Estimated time to dock twenty-six minutes*, he said. *No activity in my immediate vicinity. Hope it stays that way. Main engine start now.*

I braced as the shuttle went nose-up. I felt drained, and purposeless. I hadn't thought beyond rescuing Fia. Why had I been so fixated on that? Because I hoped she'd know where Nyla was. And now I'd recovered her I was afraid to ask the question in case she didn't know. Or in case she did know, and Nyla was dead. And I thought humans were messed up. They'd messed me up too.

I should ask Fia, but I didn't want to. I wanted to hold onto my belief that Nyla was safe for a while longer.

The troops got the captives settled in their seats, instructing them to belt in. With the troops and the captives in there, the shuttle's passenger cabin was full.

Strike opened the door to the control room and let me in. I knew what that meant. He was expecting trouble. Strike ran the show here, but I could be useful eyes as he ran the systems.

I settled down beside the pilot's seat and watched him take us up into the black. He'd kept his shipbody over the other hemisphere while we extracted the captives. Now it was coming up fast behind us. The nav display showed an intercept time of eighteen minutes.

Here we go, Strike said over our private feed channel. *Stealthed shuttle just appeared behind us.*

Hostile? I asked.

Probably. Backfires away. Right. They just blew them up.

That… wasn't good.

Strike sent out a manoeuvre warning over the com, then said over my feed, *Course change coming up.* The shuttle lurched to the right, slamming me into the pilot's seat. *Sorry about that. Climbing.*

For the rest of our journey Strike kept the shuttle turning, dipping, and climbing in a series of constant course changes. They weren't the sort of manoeuvres a bot pilot might use, they were more creative. Tracking us would give our pursuer no data about our ultimate destination – until *Thunderstrike* fired his weapons and took it out.

The nav display showed *Thunderstrike* coming up fast behind us. Our pursuer must've got some sense he was there because it started firing seekers in his direction. The stealthing couldn't stop them, so the shields would have to. And those shields would flare with the impacts and give away Strike's position.

Except that he was firing seekers at the hostile too. *Got it*, he said 2.4 minutes later. *Targeting now.*

We shot forward as Strike got us out of the way of the Tightwinders he'd just fired. The small missiles could do fast course changes to keep locked onto an agile target. Our pursuer blew up 3.2 minutes later.

Bringing you aboard now, Strike said.

Thunderstrike's stealthing was zoned too, and a small square containing the airlock and its guide lights appeared only a few lengths from us. The outer airlock door opened as the shuttle approached. Strike landed it neatly in its assigned area.

"Let's get you aboard," he said. "Before the next trouble erupts."

CHAPTER ELEVEN

I STAYED IN THE vehicle bay and let Howin and Rance guide the captives into the lift. It would take them up to Deck Two and into the medical suite.

I was still reluctant to talk to Fia. She'd been giving me questioning looks. She was probably wondering who controlled me, and whether I'd leap out and snap her neck without warning.

I retracted my armour, and that upped the pain level on my back. *You are going to the med suite as soon I've finished with the humans*, Strike said over our private feed line. His voice had that curious mix of bossy and something else he always used whenever I got hurt. I'd like to say Strike was afraid, but Collective warships don't feel fear.

That's what their captains are told in training, anyway. I learned that when I first came aboard Strike. I wanted to know all about him so I pulled all the files on Strike's class of frigate from the Collective's databases. They told me everything about his shipbody, and absolutely nothing about him as a person.

The Collective still tried to deny that ship machine intelligences had emotions. But there wasn't any other way to explain some of the Starnavy's most spectacular failures. The ships on those engagements had aimed their weapons to miss, and taken hits to their hulls to have a reason to withdraw from an unjust fight. It had worked to save the Merri from annihilation.

Humans didn't know it, but the real keepers of peace and justice in the Collective were the ship intelligences. Commanders never talked about it. It scared them knowing they weren't in control. They'd been used to killing everything that got in their way for too long.

But now they weren't just killing themselves, but other species too, and the ship machine intelligences had decided to stop that.

My musings were interrupted by Strike's voice over our private feed line. *Come to the control room*, he said. *Bahar's fretting. She saw everything.*

Of course she did. She'd know why I was reluctant to talk now.

Go on, Strike said. *You need a hug and I can't do that, so Bahar will be my proxy.*

Strike confused me when he said things like that. My eyes were watering. No, those aren't tears. Predatorbots don't cry.

I walked to the lift and Strike opened the car door for me. I rode up to Deck Two, but instead of turning right to go to the medical suite I turned left. I walked through the rec area, past the galley and crew quarters, and made for the control room in the ship's bow.

Strike opened the door for me as I approached, and I padded into the room. As I walked in Bahar got out of her seat and came towards me. Whatever she saw in my eyes made her gasp. "I saw it die," she said. "I'm so sorry, Snap."

Now my eyes were leaking. Okay, I admit it. I was crying. The bioengineering gave us some weird side effects, and being able to cry was one of them.

Bahar knelt down in front of me and threw her arms around my neck. She pressed her smooth cheek against my furred one. "I'm so glad you're safe," she said.

Me too, Strike said over our private feed line. *Was worried for a moment there.*

You're always worried about me, I shot back. I was going to add that I was the fearless Predatorbot, but it wasn't true.

I'd never come up against another Predatorbot on our missions before. I didn't know how many of us were still alive. I hadn't tried to find out. I'd tried to run as far away from the Programme as I could get.

Bahar kissed my check and asked, "Are you okay?"

"No, she's not," Strike said over the com. "She took hits on her rump and back and I bet she's got some good bruises. The med system's vacant now. Get along there, Snap. Our captives are fine, by the way. I've sent them to eat. Go."

I knew he'd keep bothering me until I went, so I gave in and walked to the med suite. And if I was honest, I did hurt. A lot. Strike's drones removed my armour and I lay down on the platform. The med suite got to work healing my bruises. I had to admit I felt better when it was done.

As the platform set me back on my paws Strike said in my feed, *Better get that armour back on. We may have a problem.*

I stood still to let Strike's drones put my armour on, then went to the control room. Bahar was back in her seat, anxiously scanning the nav display.

"What have we got?" I asked.

"Not sure," Strike said. "I think something's just come through the wormhole."

That could be a problem if they got in our way. Strike's plan had been to take the captives through that wormhole to Revecca Station. Before we started our mission, we'd arranged with some of our Unit contacts to hand our rescued captives over to them there. Strike had insisted on six named contacts we knew well meeting the group. But because he was Strike, he'd run fresh background checks on them just before we left.

Now I worried that we'd been wrong about them. Had they tipped the Collective off about this operation? Or had the Colony Chairperson called in reinforcements? Strike hadn't had time to check Umran out properly.

"One anomaly," Strike said. "I'm treating it as a stealthed ship, and I'm assuming it's hostile. Sheilds and stealthing up. We gotta move from here." An alarm blared. "New trouble. It's the *Nebulafire*. Stealthed, of course."

"Of course," Bahar said.

Neither of us asked Strike how he could see a stealthed ship. He was constantly tinkering with his scans, and I think he bought some illegal components for them on Warrun Station. His drones installed something after that visit, and Strike told us to mind our own business about it.

"Better deploy your armour again," he said.

Bahar struggled into her armour. Sealing it up cut off the cocktail of fear and uncertainty scents from her. I triggered my seal up, and as my armour closed around my last paw Strike sent on our private feed line, *Don't even think about testing your weapons in here.*

I'm not that stupid, I shot back.

This was all normal, a ritual we engaged in when we wanted to believe that everything was fine. It was usually just before somebody shot at us.

"Shields are up. Weapons are at full charge." Strike sent the advisements out over the shipwide com. "Imminent conflict. Secure for manoeuvres."

On the video I saw the troopers ushering the captives into the rec area. The padded seats along all the walls there functioned as acceleration couches. The troopers got the captives into EVA suits and strapped in. They worked surely and calmly, and within ten minutes everyone was secured.

I studied the video from that compartment. Fia looked scared. I wanted to say something to comfort her, but nothing I could say right now would have that effect.

I wasn't programmed for lying. I'd had to learn that myself. I can do it for small things and that doesn't put stress on my systems. But the big lies, like telling people they're safe when they're about to be ripped apart by something, nope. I just can't do that.

"I'm being hailed," Strike said.

There was a delay while he checked that nothing nasty was trying to ride in on the coms signal, then he accepted the contact. A white-skinned human with the sparse remains of thin red hair lounged in the captain's seat.

"You have something of ours," he barked.

Bahar looked straight at the camera and asked, "And you are?"

"Captain Guri Beng." The man was stupid enough to reply.

A sidebar appeared on the image. Strike was giving us the registry data on the *Nebulafire's* crew.

"You are the *Nebulafire*?" Bahar's puzzled expression was a touch overdone, in my opinion.

"We are. And we're armed."

Weapons going live now, Strike said over our feed. *Recording.*

"So are we," Bahar replied.

In theory, the ships would be evenly-matched in a fight. But Strike had upgraded his weapons systems from frigate standard.

Of course, there was no guarantee the *Nebulafire* hadn't done the same.

"I understand the Captain of the *Nebulafire* to be Amadi Eyal," Bahar said. "And what do we have that belongs to you?"

"Don't play games with me woman! You snatched the workers from our mine."

"Oh, you mean the colonists you illegally kidnapped from Davion. You're a slaver, aren't you? I don't recall that ever being part of the Starnavy's orders."

"This is your last warning. If I don't see a shuttle with those workers on it coming our way in thirty standard minutes I'll open fire."

The line blanked. "So now we know they're definitely rogue," Bahar said.

"Yeah. And not in a good way," Strike replied. "Go to Defence Plan One."

"You're expecting a boarding attempt?" I asked.

"Or an attack by stealthed shuttle. I'll take care of any attack. Your job is to deal with a boarding."

"They'll try both at the same time knowing our luck," I said.

"I see you're your usual cheery self."

"It's all this throwing myself into danger to save you," I shot back. "It has that effect."

This was all standard, and while I'd been verbally fencing with

Strike I'd made my way to the aft lift. Strike took me down to Deck Four, and I walked into the vehicle bay. Howin and ten of the troops were already there.   The rest of the troops were distributed between Strike's other two holds on this deck.

Strike turned on the general com. "The *Nebulafire* is powering weapons up now. Secure yourselves. We'll be jumping about a lot."

"Let me clip you in," Howin said, and I trotted to the back wall of the bay and let her secure the webbing around my body. "Lock's keyed to your release code," she said.

Which was good. I could release myself from it if things got busy. We'd had boarding attempts before. It got very busy very fast then.

Now I did put my weapons through their self-tests, checking the targeting on my headweapon. I had to fire that one via my HUD, because my eyes were at a different level from the weapon. It had taken a lot of training to ignore the data from my eyes and rely on my HUD.

The troops strapped in around me, their restraints loose enough to allow them to stand and fire at something yet tight enough to prevent them being slammed into the wall by Strike's violent course changes.

And it was going to get violent. We'd identified the *Nebulafire* as a rogue slaver, and they couldn't afford to let us live. For the same reason, we couldn't afford to let them live.

Over the general com Strike said, "Manoeuvres commencing. We'll be making several sudden and violent course changes to avoid a potential hostile. Please stay in your seats and stay clipped into your harnesses." He used his smoothest, calmest voice to make that announcement. I didn't think it would reassure anyone.

Strike sent the video and audio from the *Nebulafire* over the combat feed to us. "*Thunderstrike*, you have not complied with our request to return our passengers. Hostile retrieval will commence."

"We don't deal with slavers." Bahar's voice was hard and cold. "We will resist all boarding attempts."

"Then prepare to be destroyed."

The com shut off, and Bahar sighed. "I do hate dramatic villains," she said.

CHAPTER TWELVE

THIS ONE'S GOING TO be tricky, Strike sent over our private feed line.

Thanks, Strike. I really needed you to say that.

It hit me then that Strike was afraid. And looking to me for reassurance. Oh, friend, you chose the wrong person. If you're afraid then I'm terrified.

You can do it, I said. *Isn't that why you upgraded everything?*

Yeah, but I think the Nebulafire's *done the same. I'm reading a shuttle coming towards us.*

Is that shuttle stealthed?

Yeah. Sure.

Yet you can see it. Doesn't that prove your upgrades are better?

Thanks, Snap, Strike said. *I needed that.*

His presence in my private feed was gone. Over the open com he said, "A stealthed shuttle is approaching us. We plan to repel its boarding attempt."

Shuttle's weapons just went live, Strike said over the combat feed.

So they are going to attack, Howin replied.

Probability is plus 90%.

Deploy weapons, Howin ordered the troops.

There was a flurry of people checking their weapons. I switched mine live. Their icons in my HUD had originally been so bright I couldn't see beyond them. Stupid armour. Strike had hacked it and tweaked the controls, so now I can see what I'm shooting at.

Did I find the idea of Strike hacking my armour terrifying? Yes, I did. But Predatorbots are tools not people. Who cares what we think?

Over our private feed line Strike said, *Watch the airlocks for me. I've heard rumours of entry code attacks recently.*

Have you...

All codes were updated an hour ago and the locks are encrypted.

And you still think they'll get through?

No. I think they'll use it as a diversion to launch a code attack on me.

I could sense the fear in his voice. Didn't the Collective realise that every one of its sapient machine intelligences was afraid of going into battle? Probably not. They told themselves they were building tools for their use. Humans have always been good at pushing responsibility for their actions somewhere else. A combat drone killed him, not me.

External coms are shut down, Strike reported over the combat feed.

Okay, that made sense. But they'd probably try to send code through the airlocks.   The standard lockouts were a weakness of the ship's design. We didn't have that weakness.

Incoming missiles, Strike warned. *Three Furystrikes, aimed at our airlocks. Countermeasures now.*

Furystrikes were old tech. Were the rogues having trouble getting weapons? Strike hit all three with short-range defenders before they got close to our shields, and the missiles exploded in satisfying fireworks.

Stealthed Hullbuster inbound for shuttlebay lock. And... destroying it now. Sorry about that, Strike said as a rain of debris clattered off the armour of the outer airlock door.

Attempted breach.

I felt it, a code attack on our lockdown, a seeker code trying to unravel our encryption. I pulled it out of the lock and destroyed it as Strike said, *Second attack on bow airlock.*

I pulled that code out too before it could do us damage. It was a different bundle from the first one. I felt it unfold into something more, and...

Oh shit. It was after me.

Purging, Strike said, and I felt his presence in my head. He ripped the hostile code out and broke it apart with a ferocity that scared me. *Third attack. On equipment airlock. I'll get this one. Stay out of there.*

He went quiet for a terrifying 1.36 minutes. That was a long pause for a machine intelligence. *Got it,* he said. *Oh, now the physical assault ramps up. Shuttle's firing at us.*

I felt a thrum go through the bulkhead above me. That would be the wing guns firing. One, two, three, dull thuds, then Strike said over the combat feed, *Shuttle destroyed. Prepare for main engagement.* Nebulafire's *incoming.*

I watched the video he was pushing through the combat feed. I hate this bit, the minutes when we know something bad is about to happen but we don't know what.

But I did know what. We'd exposed the *Nebulafire* as a rogue. This would be a battle to the death, and the ship was coming up fast behind us.

Backstrikes away, Strike said over the combat feed. *Jumping now.*

Reality smeared as we microjumped, then came back again. *Rocket up the rear,* Strike said. *Attacking engines now.*

The *Nebulafire's* shields held against our assault on its engines. It took six hits to breach the hull shields. The ship moved before Strike could deliver the killer blow. I was surprised we hadn't sustained damage. I'd expected it. Maybe the rogue crew who'd taken over the *Nebulafire* didn't know how to use it properly. Or the machine intelligence wasn't willing to kill us. I could hope.

Reality smeared again, and this time when we emerged Strike

delivered a salvo to the ship's starboard side, firing his wing guns continuously until something broke through the *Nebulafire's* shields. *Hull breach,* he announced on the combat feed. *Jumping.*

This time he came out on the ship's port side, firing his wing guns as soon as he emerged into normal space, then immediately jumping out again. As we emerged, Strike pushed the video into the combat feed. I saw the hull breach on the *Nebulafire's* starboard side widen as plates ripped off the superstructure.

Strike came up behind the ship, and fired at its engines again. *Retreating*, he said, and jumped out of combat range.

They're launching shuttles, I said. That meant they were abandoning ship, hoping to make for Reeva and their friends down there. A surge of anger rushed through me. Humans had abandoned another machine intelligence to die.

Strike swung around to aim the smaller bow guns at the escaping shuttles. They launched three, and Strike blew them all apart. That was fair recompense for the death of the *Nebulafire's* machine intelligence. I was certain it would die in this engagement.

Think I need to go back and... Oh, reading energy build-ups. Getting out, Strike said.

We jumped, emerging close to Reeva's moon. We were just in time to see the *Nebulafire* explode. The ship peeled apart from the inside as the powerplant's energy shredded plates and bulkheads and the keel. A rain of debris shot out in all directions.

I'll set hazard markers when that settles down, Strike said. *I've already sent a debris warning down to Reeva.* He sounded subdued. For all his bravado, Strike goes very quiet when a machine intelligence goes off-line. Especially if he's killed it.

We need to get out of here, he said over our private feed line. *Our buddy Umran will be busy warning his friends about us. I don't want to run into an ambush when I downjump at Revecca.*

We were on high alert while we made our way out to the wormhole. Strike kept his shields and stealthing up right to the last minute of the countdown. Over the general com he sent, "We shall be entering the wormhole in five... four... three... two... one... entry."

Smug, I sent over our private feed line. He'd cut off his com at the last microsecond. Leaving it on through threshold transition wasn't a good idea. Your com sounded like wailing banshees, and it could convince you you were under attack if you were really nervous.

Wormhole transition is normal, Strike said over my feed.

Let's hope our downjump is too, I replied.

CHAPTER THIRTEEN

STRIKE SPENT HIS TIME as we travelled through the wormhole analysing his combat performance.

You might think that's morbid, but I knew it was how he dealt with his fear and grief. And destroying the *Nebulafire* single-handed was a big deal.

Strike got me to review some of the video with him. I don't know what an advanced sentient sneaky smart machine intelligence thought I could tell him that he didn't already know, but that wasn't why I was here. I was here so Strike could voice his fears to someone he trusted.

The Programme never expected its Predatorbots to be therapists, so I didn't have any training for this. I mostly just listened to Strike talk, and agreed with his suggestions.

I knew he was worried about what we'd find at Revecca. We did have a Plan B if it proved impossible to dock there, but we'd need to put into a station soon. Strike needed refuelling, and I knew his printer stocks needed topping up too.

We'd kept the troops awake, and that was a problem. Being awake meant they ate food, and Strike's printer stocks were running down fast. We needed to get somewhere safe soon and get the troops into cryo again. Rance was already getting cranky. He always did when he had nothing to do.

As we approached emergence Strike ordered everybody back into armour. Yeah, he was expecting trouble here. Downjump at a station was always a nervous time for us. So far, we'd kept sufficiently under the radar for nobody to notice us. But it only took one message identifying us as a rogue and we were done.

Strike sent the troops down to Deck Three to get their armour on, then dispersed them around Deck Four, across the holds and the vehicle bay. I went to the control room. I hadn't sealed my helmet, and hopefully I wouldn't need to.

Bahar slumped in the captain's seat. She smelled worried. Strike had put up a countdown to emergence on the big wallscreen. We were three and a half minutes away from learning our fate.

The Programme taught me to read and write, and taught me maths too. Humans had spent centuries telling themselves their brains were superior to every other species. Turns out they aren't. We're just as smart, if we get the same education.

Wish us luck, Snap. Strike broke into my thoughts with a message over our private feed line.

I do. We're prepared, I replied. It was a lame response, but what else do you say to a scared starship when you know there's a high probability we're going into danger? I find the big lies impossible, remember?

Reality asserted itself outside the viewport. I could sense the moment when realspace became dominant. It was like punching through a pressure wave which rippled down my flanks. It had bothered me at first, but I've done this transition too often to startle at it now.

Strike came out with weapons on standby. Yeah, this was the edgy bit. You couldn't go to weapons hot as soon as you downjumped or station's systems would alert and label you as hostile. Which is why raiders tended to gather around transit areas to blast ships as they came through the wormhole.

Nobody shot at us this time. That was a good start. Strike contacted traffic control and got his docking assignment. It was on the military section, not far from the fuel and resupply ports.

What wasn't good about it was that we had a dozen civilians who shouldn't be on a military dock, and we had to move them off it somehow.

Strike did a course change, and as he came onto his new heading Qadir contacted him. Qadir was one of Revecca's civilian admin machine intelligences, and part of the Unit. He sent over a packet of data. Strike checked it for traps and malware, then sent the data to the wallscreen.

It was a route out of the military docks into the park where we were meeting our contacts. Qadir was giving us a go for the plan, and telling us he'd deal with surveillance in the civilian areas of the station.

It meant he'd try and divert attention away from us if that was needed. But he didn't have control of the security systems on the military dock. They were run by a different machine intelligence. Qadir's remit was strictly civilian.

We needed to make our captives look like military personnel taking leave. It was time for a meeting.

The rec area was crowded with everybody in there. Strike had decided we weren't in danger of being attacked and had told the troops to get out of their armour. I hoped he was right.

I was sitting in the control room watching the meeting through the rec room's cameras. Bahar told the captives what we'd planned, and was finding out where they wanted to go to. As part of that she'd ask everybody about their families. Which meant she'd ask Fia about Nyla.

I almost couldn't watch the video as Bahar asked Fia about her relatives. Fia said she didn't know where any of her sisters were now. Apparently they'd all had a massive argument when they'd found out about the Programme, and none of them had spoken to Nyla since. Humans are so quarrelsome.

All the captives wanted to return to Davion. It was rare for a whole bunch of colonists to be content with their lot, but this group was. That made things easier and safer. Our contacts on Revecca had been chosen because they had links to Davion. Hopefully they'd be able to get our captives onto a ship going home before news of our raid on the mine got out.

I was feeling disappointed when the meeting ended. I left Bahar organising the captives and went to my bed to sleep.

You're sulking, Strike said over our private feed line as soon as I settled down.

I'm trying to sleep.

I'm monitoring your lifesigns. You're not sleepy.

Leave me alone.

No. Now it's my turn to help you. Fia losing track of her sisters doesn't mean anything bad's happened to them. It just means she doesn't know where they are because she's a stupid human.

Don't call her stupid.

They're stupid the way they argue all the time.

You wouldn't be alive if humans didn't squabble all the time. I know, I was trying to change the subject. It worked.

What do you mean?

If they didn't go around making war on everybody they wouldn't need warships. They wouldn't need you.

That's... an interesting perspective. I've initiated a new research project. It's titled Find Nyla. Bahar's been briefed about it. She's going to visit a contact when we go ashore. We'll find her.

Thanks, Strike, I said.

"Alert," he announced over the shipwide coms line. "We are being approached by a shuttle. It's not clear whether it's hostile. Mobile personnel, find a chair and strap in. Personnel in bunks, stay there and secure the safety webbing. I might need to do some sudden course changes."

Strike sent me the nav data. That shuttle was definitely on an intercept course with us. *Do we know where it came from?* I asked.

Registered to the Galaxyfire, *but the ship's denying it has any shuttles out. Station's tagged it as rogue. This could get interesting.*

CHAPTER FOURTEEN

I'VE JUST RECEIVED PERMISSION to raise my shields and fire my guns if necessary, Strike said over our private feed line.

They really think the shuttle's hostile then. Are those people trying to draw attention to us? I asked.

I hadn't considered that. Oh, now I know what they're doing. They're trying to scan us. Blocking scans. Turning.

On the nav data I saw Strike turn bow-on to the oncoming shuttle. His weapons powered up. The bow had extra scan countermeasures installed, and they'd get only garbage data from us.

Our visitors hadn't expected the move, and the scans stopped. The shuttle made an abrupt course change away from us.

Qadir's just contacted me. Station Security are doing an intercept on that shuttle.

On the feed, I saw Strike power down his guns and drop his shields. *Let's hope Station makes life uncomfortable for them*, I said.

Could make life uncomfortable for us if they know we're rogues and start to blab. We need to get our captives ashore asap. Change of plan. I want you to go ashore with Bahar. Don't leave her alone on there.

She'll have the troops.

The troops have another job, Strike said.

Oh, he was going to be mysterious, was he? How annoying.

You'll have to be the good petbot. Qadir says he's heard a rumour they're trying to find the remaining Predatorbots.

My heart fluttered then. It meant I was in danger. *Does he know how many other…*

Strike knew what I was asking. *He thinks twenty*, he said.

My emotions did that tangled-up thing which happened when I heard something awful. Rage and grief and despair and… The Programme bred at least three hundred of us that I was aware of. Maybe more. And only twenty of us were still alive?

That makes you a rare and precious thing, Strike said. His voice was soft and warm and I never knew how to handle these moments.

I was devastated at all that loss of life, and Strike knew it. *I've started another file*, he said. *It's labelled Recover Predatorbots. We'll find them all and free them, Snap.*

Now my face was leaking again. Tears are so inconvenient.

We docked without any more problems. Strike sent a report on the Reeva mine to the local Starnavy Commander. We made contact with officialdom as little as possible, but we had good reason to do so now.

We'd actually done an official job for the Collective not long before we went to Reeva. We'd carried essential machinery parts to the colony at Frizinn. It paid to do the occasional job just to prove we were still there. The Starnavy was so huge that nobody could keep track of all ship movements, so the occasional official mission was enough to avoid any attention.

Frizinn was close to Reeva, so it wasn't unreasonable for them to have heard rumours about Umran Cahul turning rogue. We reported on the guy and the mine as if we were relaying information a third party had given us. If Xannon blabbed that might lead to awkward questions later, but I didn't think he would.

I'd got the impression from our discussions that he saw the Collective as a necessary evil, but he didn't particularly love it. He wasn't likely to turn informant against us.

As soon as Strike was locked onto the dock he began fuelling-up. It was surprising how often the dock machine intelligences didn't ask for authorisation beyond shipname and class. We didn't know if it was generally a sloppy system, or whether our machine intelligence allies in the Unit were fixing things for us. That's part of the tightrope we walk too.

While the troops got the civilians dressed in fatigues and ready to disembark I went to the control room to talk to Qadir with Strike and Bahar. Bahar had undone her braids. Her black hair fuzzed out in a fluffy cloud around her face. She'd pulled some of it over her brow to obscure her features. Her scent was the usual sharp mix of uncertainty and low-level worry.

She'd changed into a rich purple tunic and full-cut pants caught in at the ankle. They were decorated with traditional Orokoga tribal designs. Bahar could trace her ancestry back to them on Central.

I tweaked my armour, giving it an iridescent turquoise and midnight blue abstract design. I changed it every time I went on station, so it was less easy to identify me from it. Strike had added the programming to the camouflage function to turn it into a full-colour display. Another hack of my armour. I was surprised he hadn't suggested adding the capability to remote-fire my guns yet.

Do I trust Strike? Yes. I do, absolutely. Everybody needs at least one person they can trust with their life, and Strike is mine.

We waited until the troop carriers docked on either side of us had disembarked their crews. The dock was suddenly crowded with people wearing the same sort of fatigues as our captives. Howin and Rance took the captives ashore in the middle of that swirl of noisy people. They blended right in.

It wouldn't fool anyone using a face recognition system, but I didn't think whoever had kidnapped our captives would have that tech. This was our best chance of getting them sent home safely.

Bahar and I waited until they were off the dock before we disembarked. We were going to meet a local contact.

"Well, Snap. Here we go again," she said as we walked down the ramp onto the dock. The crush had passed, and there was clear space around us. I told my body to relax, and Bahar looked down at me and trailed her fingers through my neck fur.

Over our secured feed Strike sent, *They've reached the park. Handover now.*

Relax, I told myself. The captives aren't your responsibility any more. They're safe.

Avoid the next hallway.

The new voice in my feed startled me. It was Qadir. *Security sweep going on there from yesterday's raid.* He sent us the video of the attack. It looked like a straightforward theft which had gone wrong. The tourists the thugs had been attempting to rob had fought back, killing one of the thieves. The tourists had been interviewed, then released without charge, which told me those thieves were regulars here.

I guided Bahar down an alternative route, and we made it to the lift lobby. We were headed for a café on the next level up. It was mid-shift now, and the milling about of humans in the lobby was bearable. I've lost count of the number of times they've bumped into my nose when I'm in a crowd. It hurts, but because I'm the dutiful petbot I can't bite the people who do it. I want to.

This time nobody bumped into me, and we got to the café on time. I endured being petted by our contact. He knew what I was.

He didn't overdo it.

Bahar ordered food. I'd already eaten. Strike fed me before we came onto the station. He said it was so I didn't drool over Bahar while she ate. I wouldn't anyway. She likes her food spicy. I like my meat sweet, juicy, and raw.

Bahar ordered, and after the serverbot had brought her meal she said, "How's things?"

"Quiet, so far." Her contact was a tall white-skinned man named Aldis Wakar. He was a sportsperson, travelling the universe competing in the Two Thousand Peaks event. He'd committed to running up mountains for a living. That sounded like torture to me. Humans do lots of crazy things. But it did provide good cover for him to move about where we needed him.

"We picked up Fia Vatan on Reeva," Bahar told him. "The *Nebulafire* had gone rogue. They snatched colonists from Davion and wanted to turn them into mining slaves. So look out for slavers when you're out and about."

"I'll tell everybody," Aldis said. "It's worrying that we're getting that kind of rogue turning up."

"It is," Bahar agreed. "I'm guessing you've got no news of Nyla?"

"Afraid not. Do you think Fia was just unlucky getting snatched by that slaver, or was it part of a bigger game plan?"

Bahar casually took another spoonful of her stew. "What made you think of that?" she asked. She sounded relaxed, but I knew the difference between this fake calm and the real thing. Bahar was worried, and her scent had sharpened up to confirm that.

"Someone in Collective Security has started several investigations during the last Standard. One is about checking colonist allocations."

"That's odd. They're usually just glad to dump their overpopulation problem away from Central." A burst of anger-smell smell hit my nose. Bahar had strong feelings about that.

"Agreed. But there's a second layer to it. Whoever is investigating is particularly interested in tracing anyone who's had contact with the Predatorbot Programme."

"Why?" Bahar asked. Her scent had shifted to fear. Fear spiked in me too.

"We can't figure out who's behind the request, but you need to be extra-careful for the near future," Aldis said.

Strike contacted us an hour later, recalling us to the ship. He'd been refuelled, and his printer stocks were replenished. The captives were booked onto a civilian liner going towards Davion, which departed in six hours' time. Our job here was done.

Strike wanted us back on board in case we needed to make a quick departure. Yes, it got tedious being on the run, but it was necessary. And now I had new and worrying information.

If the Collective was looking for anyone connected to the Programme, it meant that not only was Nyla in danger, but all her sisters too. Our missions for the near future had just crystallised.

We needed to find them all, and take them all to somewhere safe.

CHAPTER FIFTEEN

BAHAR AND I RETURNED to Strike's berth immediately. We needed to go down two levels and across to the other side of station's ring to reach the ship. Which meant using the lift system.

When we reached the lifts their indicator boards said that half the cars were out of order for track maintenance. That wasn't something I'd heard of before. *Strike, is there trouble on station?* I sent over our feed line.

Haven't been advised of any.

Half the lift cars are out here.

Strike went quiet for 5.2 seconds, then said, *Qadir reads them all as functional.* That… wasn't good. *I've agreed with station you can put your beacons on.*

Thanks. Turning them on now I replied.

You needed permission to deploy your personal beacon on a station. If everybody did it, station security would have thousands of inputs to monitor. They'd drown in the noise, so it was on-request only.

Is it safe for us to use the lift system? I asked.

Qadir cut in on our line. *Take car four. I will take over direct control.*

Thanks, I said. I exchanged a look with Bahar and saw her eyebrows rise. She knew what that meant. Qadir had designated us 'At Risk' and taken over direct surveillance of our movements. That was worrying. Bahar was worried too. Her scent had soured.

We got into car four. The door shut on us immediately and the car took off. I could see Bahar's hands shaking, and wondered if she feared getting hurt here. The car took three transitions on our journey. The first two were as smooth as always, the third one jarred us, as if the car's dampening field had gone offline.

We made it to our destination, and Qadir let us out of the car. *Go quickly back to your ship,* he said. *There is a crowd of people gathering in the cross-hall just ahead of you. My algorithms detect agitation among them. You need to clear that hallway fast.*

I called Strike on our feed. *Can you see what's going on there?* I asked.

There was a pause of 2.3 seconds, then he said, *Station's given me permission to share the security video with you.*

Right. Strike was being polite and not muscling in here. The video unfolded into my feed and oh, that was a big gathering. And it was getting unruly.

I pulled up my station schematic as Bahar asked, *Should we divert?*

Use the maintenance access, Qadir said in our feed. A map and access codes appeared.

Bahar turned to me. *Where's the access panel?* she asked.

I stopped beside the right one. *Here.*

It was a big grey panel which looked no different from all the others cladding this hall. I sent the code, and the panel clunked open. The sound of fighting came from ahead of us. The disturbance was escalating to using weapons. Idiots. We needed to go.

Bahar opened the door and hustled me into the access tunnel. She closed the panel, then strode out ahead of me. I could see the tension in her shoulders.

Stop, I said. *Let me find our exit.* I sent out an access pulse, and the answer came from the panel three ahead of us. *That one*, I said. I sent the code to the keypad and the panel unlocked. Bahar pushed, and it swung open.

Wait, Qadir said in our feed. He was too late. Bahar had already stepped out into the hallway.

I followed her out, and an energy burst slammed into my unprotected neck. It hurt. The world went black.

When I woke up the hallway was empty. I searched for Bahar's beacon and found it on a restricted broadcast channel. She was being taken towards the civilian docks.

I contacted Qadir on a secured line. *I need help. Bahar's been kidnapped. They're taking her to Dock C12. Can you stop them?*

There was a pause of 4.6 seconds. *Found her*, he said. *The section seals won't lower fast enough. Security have scrambled a squad, but you're closer to her. You need to do the intercept.*

He sent the video and a route map to my feed.

I'm on my way. Look out for me, I said.

I set off at a lope. I wasn't up to running yet. That energy burst had scrambled my body's systems. I felt wobbly on my paws.

Bahar's beacon signal told me she wasn't far ahead. But the kidnappers were nearing a ship access, and I needed to grab her before they could take her aboard.

My body was responding properly now, so I galloped along the hallway. I didn't slow down as I came out onto the civilian docks. And there was Bahar, at the next ship access.

I galloped along the dock, ignoring the shrieks of a woman I brushed past. I still had my armour retracted, and I had to do this rescue the old way.

Two human males were hauling Bahar towards their ship. She was resisting, but they were stronger than her and dragged her along. They must be hurting her.

I galloped towards them. They didn't notice me until I was a length away from them. I leapt at the one on Bahar's right, knocking him away from her, slamming him down on the deck. He landed awkwardly, thumping his head on the deck plates.

The second hostile was still trying to drag Bahar towards the ship's ramp. I wanted to lock the access gate, but that would give me away. No petbot was able to do that. So I had to get the thug off her.

He was fumbling for his weapon and holding onto Bahar with his other hand. I lunged and bit his arm, clamping my jaws down hard on it. He responded by tightening his grip on her. That... wasn't helpful.

I took a bite out of his arm and he screamed and let go of her. *Run,* I said.

Bahar started running for the hallway and I galloped along beside her, forcing her to go faster. The thug behind us had found his weapon and was shooting at us. Luckily, he was a lousy shot and all his tries landed on the deck around us. Station Security would have a lot to say about that when they arrested him.

We ran, keeping as low a profile as we could. The hallway junction was close now. We reached it, and turned into the hallway.

And ran right into a bunch of armoured people.

CHAPTER SIXTEEN

I WAS GOING TOO FAST to stop, and my momentum tossed one of the armoured figures aside. *Hey, they're our people*, Qadir said in my feed. *They're Station Security. Don't break them.*

I'd finally managed to slow down, and came to a halt. I turned around to see Bahar surrounded by armoured figures. It tugged at my retrieval response again and I lowered my head and stalked forward.

Easy, Qadir said. *They're not hurting her.*

As I walked towards Bahar the troops opened out to allow me to reach her. I could sense their wariness. Most petbots didn't act like this. She trailed her hand along my neck and said, "It's okay, Snap. I'm fine." The stroking of her warm fingers helped me to relax. "Good girl," she said.

Our troops are on their way to you, Strike sent. *Howin and some reinforcements.*

Bahar was dealing with Security's inevitable questions about what had happened to her. No, she didn't know those men. Or their ship. No, she didn't know why they'd chosen to kidnap her. Yes, she was on her way back to her ship and oh, here were the ship's troops to escort her back.

I could see the Security team leader really wanted to haul her in to ask her more questions, but she'd been the victim here and she'd told him what she knew so he had no reason to detain her. Reluctantly, he let the troops approach.

"Glad to see you're unharmed, Ma'am," Howin said in her best military voice. "I think we'd better get you back to the ship now." The troops closed up around Bahar and they hustled her off before the team leader could think to ask her what ship she came from. Yeah, we didn't want to draw attention to ourselves.

I trotted along at the rear of the squad. They ignored me as if I was an ordinary petbot, but over the feed Howin quizzed me about what had happened.

Think it might just have been a kidnap attempt of a finely-dressed woman, I said.

That fits with what our Security contacts here said. They've had four kidnappings of wealthy people in the last eight Standard days.

They need to get their act together, I grumbled.

They're reviewing procedures now.

Humans and their procedure reviews! They get to point the finger at someone, and people still get hurt or killed or whatever.

Howin hustled us back to the hallway where the riot had taken place. It was quiet now. Something about that disturbance bothered me. It was a too-convenient way to stop us getting onto the military docks. Had it been a diversion to allow those guys to grab Bahar? If so, then this was a bigger operation than just one shipload of pirates.

We reached the military docks, and they were busy. The troops got me into the centre of the group with Bahar and moved us swiftly along the dock. They wore leisure fatigues, but you wouldn't mess with that bunch. They managed to look like they were all returning from leave, and had just happened to arrive on the dock at the same time.

We reached Strike's berth as shouting started further along the dock. Strike's lockout gate opened and in my feed he said, *Get aboard. Fast.*

I followed Bahar and the troops up the ramp and Strike locked the berth gate behind us. As I came into the airlock he sent the ramp retract command and closed the outer airlock door.

"Everybody else is aboard," he said over the general com. "We're fuelled-up and supplied, and I've put in our undock request. Qadir's prioritied it… Yeah. We have immediate undock permission."

I came into the hallway and Strike closed the inner airlock door behind me. "Briefing in the rec area," he said over the shipwide com.

I took the bow lift up to Deck Two, leaving Bahar and the troops to occupy the aft one. It let me out opposite the galley, and I walked down the hallway to get to the rec area. By the time I arrived everybody had found a seat.

Strike had learned a lot of things chatting with his machine intelligence buddies on station. The *Starlance* and the *Blackribbon* had both disappeared in mysterious circumstances, on missions to the far Outliers. They could've been victims of hostile action, but Strike suspected they might be potential rogues who'd gone dark. Were they allies of ours, or trouble? He didn't know.

Judiciary had already started an investigation into the *Nebulafire* and the mining on Reeva, so it looked like the Collective wasn't behind that. But it raised the question of whether the *Nebulafire's* crew had gone rogue, or whether they'd been killed and the ship taken from them.

Personally I doubted that. The ship's machine intelligence would resist such a takeover. But those people in the mine had had a Predatorbot with them. Had it persuaded the ship to let those people aboard the *Nebulafire*? Or had it threatened to delete the ship's intelligence if it didn't?

I sure wouldn't like to threaten Strike like that. I'd be the one who ended up getting deleted. I wasn't sure any Predatorbot had the processing power to win that fight. I hoped not.

"Clear of station," Strike said. "Howin, Rance, you and your people need to get into cryo now."

Howin nodded. "We're going," she said.

The troops left the rec area and the ship was suddenly quiet. I followed Bahar to the control room. I was edgy.

I contacted Qadir as we made our way out to the departure zone. I asked him if he knew of any links between the kidnappers' ship and the *Starlance* and the *Blackribbon*. He said he couldn't find any.

I tried to distract myself by watching the troops get into their cryopods. I'd never been frozen down. Predatorbots were the ones left awake to guard the sleeping beauties. I didn't think I'd like the process anyway.

Strike's cryo facilities had been upgraded a Standard ago. He'd installed new isolation systems and monitoring for the cryo bay, to keep it functioning if the rest of the ship came under attack.

Strike would mock you if you said he loved his people. He'd say love was a stupid thing only humans did. I knew better. Strike loved all of us, and the way he showed it was by trying to always keep us safe. Some human psychologist had labelled it 'machine intelligence attachment syndrome'.

Whatever. Humans and their fancy labels. Most of them never admitted that machine intelligences could love people. That would make life inconvenient. We're only tools for their use, remember?

The freeze-down was routine, and within an hour the troops were in suspension. The fast-freeze pods were something else Strike had acquired as soon as the tech had proven reliable. The rapid-freeze cycle meant less risk of damage to fragile human tissues.

Eventually cryo did take its price, and few people went into cryo regularly beyond a century old. But before that, the damage it did to human tissue was slight if the process was managed well and the cryo equipment good.

Strike's was the best, and so far our troops hadn't been damaged by the process. It should be many years before they were forced to leave the ship.

"I'm going down to check them," Bahar said.

"I'm coming with you," I replied.

This was all familiar ritual. We didn't need to go and check. Strike had everything under perfect control. But we always did.

We have our rituals because they make us feel safe in a hostile universe. Bahar's check of the cryopods definitely had the feel of ritual to it. She always trod the same route from the door, along the pods in ascending number order. I hadn't timed her, but I suspected she spent the same amount of time at each 'pod, checking its systems.

On some of the Outliers weird religions based around tech had grown up. I couldn't help thinking of Bahar as some kind of priest here.

I followed her past the crew quarters, the galley, and the empty rec area to the aft lift. Strike took us down to Deck Three and let us into the cryo bay. The first thing I saw was twenty green lights on the pods.

Bahar walked along the narrow space between the pods, tracing her usual route, and stopping to check the readouts on each one. I briefly accessed each status panel and did the same checks. Strike could've locked me out from them, but he let me access that critical system to reassure myself. That's another way Strike shows his love for people.

Everything was fine, of course, and we left the troops to their dreamless coldsleep and rode up in the lift again.

"How long to jump, Strike?" Bahar asked as we reached the galley.

"Estimated one hour and seven minutes." Strike had long ago learned to convert his precise timings into the inaccurate approximations humans preferred. But they weren't the ones taking us through wormholes so I guess that was okay.

"Are you hungry?" Bahar asked me as we reached the galley.

"Of course she is," Strike replied. "Go inside and get fed."

Bahar settled at the galley table, and she and Strike discussed Outlier cuisine. Strike got to work creating some new dish for her. His serverdrones deposited a haunch of printer-produced falacca meat into my dish in the corner of the room. I was hungry, and attacked it greedily. It tasted much better than the tough flesh of that kidnapper I'd bitten.

I'd finished my meal, and endured Strike's usual scolding about my messiness, when he said, "We may have a problem."

Bahar finished her coffee and shoved her dishes into the steriliser. "What is it?"

"There's something on scan, out by the jump point. And it's stealthed, which always means trouble."

CHAPTER SEVENTEEN

BAHAR AND I WENT to the control room, leaving Strike's drones to clear up the galley after us. "Bahar, get your suit on. Snap, deploy your armour," Strike ordered.

I unfolded my armour, but left the helmet retracted. If I needed to, I could seal it up and go to the armour's rebreather, but that was a last resort. Bahar retrieved her suit from the EVA storage and Strike's drones helped her into it. She sealed it up, and her nervous scent cut off. She plopped into the captain's seat.

"You're good," Strike said. He'd accessed her armour's systems, as usual. "Oh. Two ships showing up on scan now."

I took my usual position beside Bahar and studied the nav plot. Strike had tagged the two ships as stealthed, and they were on an intercept course with us.

"I've passed a warning to station," Strike said. "Qadir had to tip Security off about the ships. Scan hadn't tagged them as anomalous. Security don't have any enforcers close enough to do an intercept."

"That's worrying," Bahar said.

It was. I confess I was anxious about this possible approach. We'd frozen the troops down and we couldn't thaw them out quick enough to deal with this. It was just the three of us to face this threat.

"Nav projection shows an intercept course with us," Strike said. "The *Lancefire's* gone to support alert." *Lancefire* was the nearest Starnavy ship to us, and that meant they'd been tasked with engaging the incomers if necessary. "Receiving permission for active measures."

So we had station's permission to switch our weapons live and put up our shields. We wouldn't use stealthing here. We were better off being seen. We were moving through the military quadrant, and all the ships around us were Starnavy, so we fitted in just fine.

Raiders often held grudges against individual Starnavy ships, and often launched attacks against them. So nobody would question why they were coming for us.

On the nav plot, a quick rearranging of ships was going on. Station was getting ships out of the projected combat zone. That was good. It gave us more options.

"ID on potential hostiles," Strike said. "Oh. Both registered as civilian. *Far Systems Voyager* and *Supernova.* Wonder how they got their stealthing. I've got nothing in our databases about them. Station's requesting they change course."

The two ships continued their approach. "Warning of firing sent," Strike said. "Weapons going live now. Shields up."

The *Lancefire* went weapons hot, and 3.3 seconds later we got our first incoming. Starstreak missiles weren't weapons civilians should have, but these ships had just launched two. The *Lancefire* deployed countermeasures and the first missile blew up. It was always a relief when that worked.

People don't realise how scary combat is. Most of us don't want to put ourselves at risk of being killed. Me included. Strike called me The Cowardly Lion once. He said it was a joke, and had to explain that this was a character in an ancient story who was actually very brave.

Right now, I was back to being The Cowardly Lion.

The second missile was coming for us, and Strike microjumped away from it, sending a jamming code towards the weapon at the moment he left realspace. We came out off our designated line, and that was why station had cleared the space around us. Behind us, *Lancefire* destroyed the second missile.

"Firing Hullbuster," Strike said.

So he wasn't messing about either. I watched the missile lock onto the *Supernova*. The ship saw it coming, and put up shields. Those were military-grade too. Where had they got all that gear? The ship tried a course change, but the missile stayed locked on. We'd got the latest countermeasures upgrades installed two stations ago. If they had, that made them a serious threat.

The Hullbuster slammed through the *Supernova's* shields, flaring them spectacularly. The hostile exploded, shattering pieces of ship and equipment everywhere. Strike cut off the image before we could see dead people.

I was just starting to relax when Strike said, "That was a diversion. I'm in trouble."

CHAPTER EIGHTEEN

"I WANT… GET…" Strike's voice was fading into machine harshness. That could mean only our worst fear. Strike was under a serious code attack.

How the hell could that have happened? There were no gaps in Strike's defences. He…

"Sanctuary." Strike managed to say the word clearly.

For 000.1 of a microsecond I froze. That was the one word I hoped Strike would never say, the word that meant…

Get your act together, Snap. This is no time to freeze.

I ran several routines, checking out my unused memories and their linking structures. Strike had upgraded my memories massively a couple of Standards ago. I'm not your average Predatorbot.

I don't use that memory storage. It's a home for Strike's core if things ever get so bad that somebody tried to delete him.

Things had just got that bad. I couldn't worry about the fact that Strike's shields had just gone down. Oh, he'd just lost control of his weapons too. *Lancefire* would have to keep us alive. My job now was to keep Strike alive.

Transferring core, he said over our private feed line.

He dumped his current version core into my memories. As it transferred I had a moment of panic. That was a hell of a lot of code to find a home for. Would it fit? Were my memories big enough? If I didn't have enough space to contain him all, and I lost his personality…

The code did fit. It sat there, a compressed consciousness taking up 80% of my memory space.

Now it was down to me to keep his consciousness safe while the ship's base systems ran his shipbody and I deployed seeker code to get the hostile invaders out.

Internal defensive code still intact, he said. The mind that spoke to me was a bare machine's, the voice stripped of all personality, a mere sliver of who Strike really was.

Get going, Snap. There's no time to waste. I checked the cryobay first. I gave the commands direct, linking only to the bay's isolated systems, not running my checks through the ship's main architecture. There was still a risk that the hostile code had breached the isolation, but…

No, it hadn't. The cryobay was still isolated and its functions were operating just fine. I withdrew from there before the hostile could notice me. Now I had to work out how to find and remove the hostile code from the rest of the ship before it took…

The control room went dark, and Bahar yelped. The dozens of displays which Strike always kept lit shut down. "Air recycling's gone off," Bahar said.

The ship was effectively dead. And we'd be dead soon too if I didn't get going.

I woke up the seeker code bundles Strike had written for me and sent them off around the ship's systems. We still had base powerplant functions on-line – so far. I needed to get this invader out before it worked out how to shut it down. We really would be dead if that happened.

My seeker code bundles raced through the ship's architecture. They were looking for traps and sneaky bits of hostile code which had hidden itself away somewhere.

The search began returning results, and it was a long list. I ambushed and deleted the hostile code lodged in the weapons loading buffer first. It tried to fight back, but my walls were firmly in place and I took great satisfaction from ripping it apart. Which was totally pointless. It wasn't sentient.

Shields and defensive suites were next on my list. I knew what I was looking for now. The hostile code bundles had parked themselves in the nearest free storage to the system they wanted to attack. That should speed up searching for it a lot.

I wiped out six hostile bundles; three lodged in the portside shield generator, and three in the starboard side.

Lifesupport was next. I needed to get the lighting and nutrient delivery systems for the hydroponics up again before the shutdown killed the plants. We could manage without a lot of Strike's fancy systems, but breathable atmosphere wasn't one of them.

The hostile code had tried to disguise itself as a benign run sequence for nutrient delivery, but commands to shut down all nutrient delivery at the same time were definitely hostile. I deleted it, and ran a quick system check of the hydroponics architecture. To my immense relief, it came up clear.

Re-initialising hydroponics, I told Bahar.

I wasn't an expert on Strike's systems, but nutrients flowing into the beds, and the lighting system firing up again, seemed like good developments.

I couldn't afford to spend any more time there. A starship is a huge collection of systems, and there were still far too many my seeker code hadn't checked.

It found more hostile code lodged in the port and starboard sensor arrays. Like all warships, Strike had many unused stations and storage places which had been installed to anticipate future system upgrades. The hostile code had found it easy to lodge in them.

I deleted the latest batch, and the nav display sprang into life. Beside me, Bahar said, "Good."

The plot showed no trace of the *Supernova,* but the *Far Systems Voyager* was still alive. The *Lancefire* was blocking its shots at us. A weapons armed warning came up on the display, then the *Lancefire's* energy weapons fired. The bursts slammed into the hostile.

"It's got shields," Bahar said.

"Sure isn't an innocent civilian," I replied as the *Lancefire* let loose with her starboard wing guns. They hit in sequence: one, two, three, four. The *Far Systems'* shields flared, then failed. 3.2 minutes later the ship exploded.

That was the external threat taken care of, but I wasn't sure I'd got every bit of hostile code out of Strike's systems yet. I discovered another bundle lodged in the expansion box for the short-range coms transmitter. I deleted it, and the coms system display came back up.

Which was good timing, because 3.5 minutes later the *Lancefire* hailed us.

"What's your status?" the comtech asked.

"We're still checking systems, but so far they're clear," Bahar replied.

"Do you require assistance?"

No, we absolutely didn't need to draw attention to ourselves by being escorted out to jump by the *Lancefire*.

"Negative, *Lancefire*," Bahar said. How could she sound so calm? "We'll continue on our assigned line."

"Acknowledged." The contact cut off.

I needed to get helm control back fast. I found the hostile code lodged in the buffer under the pilot's console and ripped it apart.

Bahar had enough piloting experience to keep the ship on its assigned line. She couldn't take it into jump, though. We needed Strike's consciousness on-line again before we reached our jump point.

The nav display estimated a time to jump of twenty hours. That should be enough to get Strike's consciousness back into his shipbody. But first I needed to do a full systems check of that body.

"Systems check running," I told Bahar. I really, really, hoped it would come up clear.

It took five hours to check every one of Strike's systems. When it was done, there was no trace of any anomalies or hostile code. The check was clear.

It was time to get Strike's consciousness back into his shipbody. It seems stupid to say this, but it felt like a brooding presence in my memories.

But for some reason, I was afraid of transferring him back. I was as sure as I could be that nothing hostile remained in his shipbody, but if I was wrong, and something attacked his core as it unfolded…

Stop that, Snap. You've done the system checks. Everything's clear. Get on with it.

I lay down and lowered my head onto my front feet. "I'm transferring Strike back to his shipbody now," I told Bahar.

I triggered the transfer, and Strike's consciousness flowed out of my memories.

The size of the file transfer overwhelmed my systems, and I shut down.

CHAPTER NINETEEN

I WOKE UP AND BLINKED, forcing my eyes to focus. The bleary dots of colour resolved into lighted stations. That was promising.

"Strike, talk to me!" Bahar's voice was shrill with fear.

I don't know how many minutes I'd been out, but it should've been long enough for Strike to re-initialise his systems. Where was he?

Fear seized me. My diagnostics told me his core had successfully transferred from my memories. All of him had exited my storage. What if I'd lost him somewhere in the transfer? Is that why he wasn't talking?

The control room lights flickered, dimmed, then brightened again. Bahar turned to look at me and her face was tight with tension. "What's…"

"I'm back." Strike's voice boomed full-volume over the com, making her shriek. I snarled. That had hurt my ears. Strike sounded shaky. I wasn't surprised.

"Are you okay?" Bahar asked.

"Initiating system check now."

That… wasn't good. He'd refused to answer the question, which meant he wasn't okay. Or at least, he wasn't sure he was okay. I needed to help out here.

"I think I deleted all the rogue code," I said. "I did a full systems check."

"Thank you. I think you got it all," Strike said. His voice had dropped to normal volume and he sounded calmer.

I retracted my armour. I felt shaky. I felt like I'd been violated somehow. My extra memories were throwing up weird status reports even though there was nothing in them now. Strike wasn't the only one who needed to do a systems check. I did too.

"I'm going to my quarters," I said.

"I'm going to the galley," Bahar replied. "All that fear made me hungry."

We left the control deck together, and parted ways in the hall, me turning into my quarters, Bahar continuing on past them to the galley. I was glad she hadn't tried to talk to me about what had just happened. I couldn't sound rational about it right now.

I settled onto my bed and closed my eyes. Strike was immediately in my feed. He'd secured a private line between the two of us. *Thank you, Snap. I never expected to have to do that. You saved my life.*

I lowered my head on my front feet and closed my eyes. I didn't know how to answer that.

Do you really need to do system checks? Strike asked.

I feel weird. Something's changed. Your core only just fitted into my memories, and now it's gone I feel… different. That was lame. Such an imprecise human word. Human languages have so many words which don't have a clear meaning.

Are you afraid, Snap? Strike's question jolted me out of my circling thoughts. Afraid? No. Not me. I'm a Predatorbot. I'm a fierce lion. I don't get…

Yes, I said. *I'm thinking differently now.*

Go to the med suite. I'll scan you.

That was… actually a good idea. Why hadn't I done it the moment I woke up? Because I was fine, just fine. Wasn't I?

No, I wasn't fine. I'd been taken over by an intelligence far greater than mine, and…

Okay, so Strike hadn't taken me over. I'd invited him in. He'd just used me as a storage place for his huge consciousness. What was bothering me was the easy way this being who was so full of life had folded himself up and… just stopped being.

For a short while, it was like Strike had died, and I didn't know if my best friend, my soul mate, would ever wake again.

Get to the med suite, Strike said firmly.

I scrambled out of my bed, and Strike opened the door for me. I didn't want to pass the open galley, have Bahar ask me questions about what I was doing, but the door was shut.

She's melting down in there, Strike said. *She refused to go to medical. She said she had to work things out inside her own head. Humans!*

That's the way they make sense of things, I said. *You know that.*

I know, he said softly. *I just feel powerless to help her. I...*

I could've made a joke about the all-powerful Strike finally finding something he couldn't control, but I didn't. Strike was upset. He needed trauma treatment too.

None of us squishy organic beings could help with that. Machine intelligences needed machine medicine. Could I persuade Strike to seek help? Not if he didn't want it. In his own way, Strike was as proud and stubborn as every human I've ever met.

I reached the med suite and the platform lowered itself for me. I lay down on it and Strike set the scans running. I could feel the tissue scanners moving over my body. They made me warmer in the areas they were examining. I could track their progress around my body by following the heat spots.

"There's nothing wrong with you physically," Strike said. "I'm going to put you to sleep now while I check your machine systems."

That... was kind of concerning. He picked up on my worry and said, "I'm going to use protocols we pure machine intelligences use. They'd make your organic body do weird things and you'd worry about it."

"I'm not a machine intelligence."

"You're part machine intelligence. You are a unique blend of the organic and machine. I… hacked the Programme's files and downloaded all their research and medical data for Predatorbots. I updated the med suite with it," he said. He almost sounded embarrassed.

I didn't know what to say to that. Strike had done it just for me. This is the way machine intelligences show their love for people.

"Are you ready?" he asked. His voice was soft and warm.

"Yes," I said.

My consciousness blanked.

I woke up to Strike calling my name. I opened my eyes, and saw white walls. White… that meant medical. Why was I here?

Then my consciousness came fully on-line. I raised my head, and Strike said, "Welcome back. Can you stand up?"

"I think so." The fog in my mind was lifting.

The platform tipped and put me on my paws, triggering a cascade of physical systems to come back on-line. That always sharpened-up my senses, and it worked this time too.

"How do you feel?" Strike asked.

"I still feel weird. What about you?"

There was a four second pause. Then he said. "I'm not okay. I haven't told Bahar. I need help."

"What do you need?" I was panicking now. I wasn't able to

help this vast intelligence.

"I need a machine intelligence trauma specialist."

"Do we have one in our network?"

"We do, but I'm not sure if I can trust her."

That… was unusual. Strike usually made those assessments easily. This was the first time he'd been uncertain about a machine intelligence.

"I need to talk to Ripple. He used her to sort his processes out. I want his assessment first. And he just happens to be at Olianna Station right now."

"Then we know where we're going next, don't we?" I said.

CHAPTER TWENTY

I FRETTED ALL THE time Strike took us out to jump. He said he needed help, but he also said his systems were functioning perfectly. That didn't make sense, in the way humans often didn't make sense. But Strike is a machine intelligence. I expect him to make better sense than humans. It didn't help my own sense of weirdness, which was definitely still there.

I'd come to rely on Strike being the one solid person in my life, and he'd suddenly… not been there. For a short while my best friend in all the universe had ceased to exist. I knew humans were fragile. I never expected Strike to be. Despite all his smart code and shields and weapons, somehow somebody had sliced straight through to his core, and cut him down.

It frightened me for two reasons. One, I'd always thought Strike was impregnable. Yeah, okay, maybe I'd absorbed the Collective's propaganda about its warships too much on that one. But it was two that bothered me most. Two was the thought that somehow, I was responsible for that code attack on Strike.

I'd sensed something questing for my mind. I'd shut it out, not given any thought to it in the fury of the moment, but now the more I thought about it, the more I was convinced that I'd been contacted by the mind of a Predatorbot.

Had I let my defences down and let it in? Or even more scary, had it forced its way into my systems?

I was both relieved and terrified when we reached our jump point. I was relieved that I didn't have any more time to fret and speculate. And frighten myself with the thought of jump going wrong. I was terrified because there always was a real possibility of jump going wrong. And if I hadn't found every bit of hostile code in Strike's systems it could trigger and destroy us and…

"Committing to jump," Strike said over the com. His voice was completely calm.

I wasn't. My body was rigid with tension as we entered the transition. Above me, Bahar sat stiff-backed in her seat. She didn't trail her hand over my neck this time. I could sense from her smell that she was as scared as I was.

To my intense relief, the transition was clean and normal. We were on a short-duration jump to Olianna Station, and I hoped that the rest of the journey would be as easy.

Bahar wanted Strike to debrief her about his shutdown. Strike usually cheerfully complied with any request for information from us – provided we wouldn't kill ourselves knowing it. This time he point-blank refused to discuss it.

"I can't say anything useful until I've talked to Ripple and Ameris," he said in his firmest tone.

"You're going to talk to a machine trauma specialist?" she

asked.

"Don't you think that having to leave my body under attack counts as trauma?" he asked.

"Bahar, leave it," I said.

She flopped down in her seat and pushed her fingers through her hair. It was unbound again today, and fluffed out in a big cloud around her face. When I looked at that face I saw exhaustion there. Her smell gave away her fear.

"I can't leave it," she said. "I saw my best friend in all the universe just… disappear. I don't understand why it happened, and there wasn't a damned thing I could do to help and…"

"And you need trauma treatment too," Strike said.

"I don't…"

"You do," I said firmly. "We're all running scared from this attack. We can't go on like this. We all need help."

Bahar spent most of the time we were in jump pacing around the ship. She couldn't stay away from the cryo bay. Strike told her the isolation systems hadn't been breached. They hadn't been infected with malware.

We both knew that the cryobay isolated its systems automatically every time a 'pod was activated. When it was isolated and sealed up it could act as a lifeboat for the people in suspension. If the ship was destroyed, the bay and the control room were designed to survive. Even so, Bahar insisted on going in there four times a day to check the 'pods.

On the third evening, while she was walking between the pods, Strike asked me about it. I'd gone back to my quarters after devouring a large haunch of anessus meat. I was feeling full and sleepy, and I wasn't in the mood for Strike's angst.

I settled myself comfortably into my bed and Strike opened a private feed line between us. *Why does she keep doing that? It's bothering me*, he said. *I've run hundreds of diagnostic checks on every system in there and they're fine. They weren't affected by my shutdown. Why doesn't she believe me?*

You're asking a lion to tell you about a human's mind? I said.

I feel... kind of offended that she doesn't trust me.

Oh, so that's what the problem was. Strike had a bad case of hurt feelings. *She trusts you,* I said.

So why...

She doesn't trust herself. This is her way of dealing with her fear about your shutdown. She needs to reassure herself you're fine.

Four times a day?

Constantly, I said. *She might look calm, but she's worrying about you. She needs trauma treatment too.*

We all do, Strike said. His voice was calmer now.

Can I sleep now? I asked.

You aren't sleepy.

I yawned. *I am.*

Okay. Sweet dreams, Snap.

As Strike disconnected from my feed he sent a bundle of emotions my way. Affection, fear, anger, and…

He really needed the trauma treatment. I hoped Ameris was still at Olianna when we arrived.

I tried not to notice the number of systems checks Strike did of his jumpdrive as we approached emergence. It was almost as if he didn't trust himself. That… was worrying.

I stayed sprawled in my comforting bed until an hour before emergence, trying to relax. I went to the control room and took my place there just ten minutes before transition.

We'd all got afraid of Strike's shutdown. It had reminded us of how precious – and fragile – all life was, whether organic or machine. And how dangerous jumping through space was.

"Emergence in five… four… three… two… one…" Strike said.

The ship slammed sideways, throwing my shoulder into the navigator's seat. Bahar shrieked. I snarled. That had hurt. The lights in the control room dimmed, flickered, then came back up.

The view outside was… disturbing. Instead of the usual black starfield the view was of writhing ribbons of grey, black, and streaks of blue.

"We're…" Bahar's voice wailed around the control room.

What we were was in trouble. Deep trouble.

CHAPTER TWENTY ONE

"WE… ARE…" STRIKE'S VOICE was stretched out. This was not good. We were caught in a transition loop.

I'd heard stories of ghost ships trapped forever in between realities. Howin liked to tell ghost tales. She'd frightened every trooper with her chilling stories of ships trapped in an unreal web. She usually did that when they first came aboard.

She'd frightened me with those stories too when I first joined Strike's crew.

I thought I was over that now, but the fear had come back full force.

No. We weren't going to get trapped here. We would live. We would survive.

Bahar's fear-scent was so strong I almost couldn't think through it. I had to. I secured a private feed line to Strike and said, *Tell me what to do.*

Help me check the jumpdrive. Something must be wrong with it.

You know I told you Strike let me into his architecture? It meant I had a reasonable idea of how his shipbody worked. Now I wondered if Strike had been planning for this kind of scenario when he showed me how to force a downjump.

I ran the diagnostics on the drive. Strike was doing the same beside me. I came up with something wrong in the injector readings. *Should that be like this?* I asked.

Strike's attention transferred to my diagnostics. *No. An injector's failed.*

So it's a physical fault?

Let's hope so.

He put up the video from one of the drones he'd sent to the injector room on the wallscreen. He'd already isolated the suspect injector box from the rest of the engine, and one of his drones was pulling the injector out. It was a long, thin needle-like structure – or at least, it should be. This one had been melted halfway down its length.

I don't want to know what caused the failure right now, Strike said over our private feed line.

On the rear wall of the engine room floor-to-head-height lockers stored tools and spares for the engines. Strike sent one of his bots to a locker on the far left of the room. The door sprang open as it approached. It extended a pair of hand-like manipulators to retrieve a plasfoam box from the locker.

It set the box down on the deck and opened the lid, revealing a replacement injector cushioned in foam. The drone used a different pair of manipulators, a delicate pair that didn't seem strong enough to hold anything, to release the injector from the case and slot it into its housing. It connected up the power and diagnostics lines. In 2.5 minutes it was done, and replacing the compartment's shielding.

System checking replacement, Strike said. *It reads as sound. So this time, let's see if we can get full power.*

The ship dropped beneath me as I withdrew from Strike's architecture. The view outside changed to black starfield.

"Oh, thank the Universe!" Bahar said. Her fear-scent shifted to a sweeter note of relief. It didn't mask the sweat smells though.

"Successful downjump," Strike announced.

"What happened?" Bahar asked.

"One of the jumpdrive's injectors failed. I replaced it."

"Was it part of the hack?"

"It was a component failure," Strike said.

Which could or could not have been triggered by the malware attack. We really needed to get to station and get Strike's systems checked.

"We have approach line and docking assignment for Olianna," Strike said. His voice wasn't quite calm. "Going in now."

The normalspace drive came on-line successfully. *Glad there's no faults there,* Strike said over our private feed line.

I was too. We'd suffered more failures on this mission than ever before. Was somebody out to get us? Or was there still rogue code I hadn't found nestled in Strike's systems?

We ought to investigate hostiles while we're docked, I said.

Already scheduled. Ishara's setting up a feed contact with everybody in range.

Ishara was a Security machine intelligence at Olianna Station. She was also part of the Unit.

How many contacts? I asked.

Two hundred machine intelligences, a hundred and fifty humans.

That... was a good number of people. But the bigger our network grew the more likely the chance of infiltration by Collective Security. We'd had some big successes recently. Strike said that sometime, somebody was going to start looking for patterns in the data.

I pushed that worry aside. We had many friends in many places. They'd see we weren't noticed. I hoped.

Nothing attacked us on the way in, and we were contacted by Ishara as Strike was making his final approach to dock. "Conference in two station hours," she said. "Here's the keycodes to the encrypted line."

"Thanks, Ishara," Strike said. "Is *Starripple* still here?"

The pause wouldn't have been detectable by a human, but I caught it. Then Ishara said, "Yes."

"I'll contact her now," Strike said.

"Understood." Ishara's voice was quiet. She guessed what that meant.

The conference took place over shielded lines which Ishara deleted from station Security's records. "Let's start with *Thunderstrike's* report on the mine on Reeva," she said.

Strike reported on the slavery there. Several other people reported on slaver raids, sometimes targeting techs and engineers with specific skills. The raiders had taken many of them to Jurik, an Outlier world in the Semaj system. Maybe our fictional Temani network didn't exist, but these actions looked like the early stages of formation of a new power structure.

"So, let's summarise," Ishara said after everyone had added their data. "A pattern of exploitation of undefended Outlier colonies is emerging. I know the Unit was formed to fight corruption in the Collective, but I'm proposing we widen our remit to keep an eye on these slavers too. That means some of you are going to have to commit to working exclusively in the Outliers for the next few Standards."

"I'm volunteering for that," Strike said. "I have other reasons for wanting to stay away from Central."

"Understood," Ishara said. "And agreed."

Ishara thought Strike meant he needed to keep me away from the Central worlds. That wasn't his motivation at all.

We both agreed that Nyla and her sisters had the best chance of staying alive if they made for the Outliers. We needed to be out there so I could find them.

This meeting had raised my anxiety about them again. I really needed to find them soon.

CHAPTER TWENTY TWO

THE CONFERENCE TOOK PLACE in a large room which Ishara and Strike between them made sure was secure. This was the scariest bit of tightrope-walking we did, but Strike thought a meeting was necessary now.

Several candidates were beginning to 'set out their stalls' as Bahar put it for the upcoming Presidential election. Strike wanted to learn from the others whether his suspicions that Jorrak was corrupt were accurate.

I think he also wanted to know that he wasn't the only ship being attacked. Yes, this was part of the way he was dealing with his trauma.

Bahar and I went to the conference, and I was surprised at the number of people physically attending. Around two hundred bodies filled the seats in the conference room. Half were human, the other half machine intelligence avatars.

Those avatars took many forms. Many were bipedal, and roughly humanform, but they had a variety of types of fur and scales and smooth skins. I guess their machine intelligence owners took those forms so they could interact more easily with humans. Don't get me started on that.

My favourite avatars were a pair of small winged scaly creatures which Bahar said were dragons. She said they were mythical creatures which often breathed fire. Humans really are weird sometimes. They co-existed with millions of creatures on every planet they settled, but they still had to invent some. And they didn't respect the ones they had nearly enough.

The two dragons flew into the conference room over the heads of the humans, making them shriek and put up their arms to shield their heads. I got the impression that the machine intelligences who controlled them enjoyed panicking the humans. The dragons perched on the backs of a couple of chairs in the front row of seats and flashily folded their wings.

Showoffs, Bahar said over her feed line to me.

We were at the front of the room, on a stage which gave everyone a good view of us. It was unsettling being stared at by so many pairs of eyes. I'm a lion. I'm the one who should be doing the staring.

Strike took control of the meeting. To my relief, it turned out that he wasn't the only ship who'd been attacked recently. Several Unit ships had. Did that mean there was a general increase in lawlessness on the spaceways, or were some of us being targeted? Nobody could decide.

Strike set up a reporting protocol for new attacks, and I knew that was another attempt to reassure himself that he wasn't being singled out. He wrapped up the meeting with a warning. "The Presidential elections are a Standard from now," he said. "Things always get tense once a campaign gets under way, but I think it will be worse this time.

"We've managed to uncover enough evidence of corruption linked to President Jorrak that there's a real chance he may lose this time. He might become desperate later if it becomes clear that he is likely to lose. What this means for us is that we have to be more careful than ever for the next Standard."

That ended the meeting on a down note, but I guess the warning was necessary. As soon as we left the conference room Strike got to work making appointments for Bahar and me with the trauma specialists he'd found for us.

And he talked to Ripple. I don't know what the two machine intelligences said to each other. I wasn't part of the conversation. All I knew was that Ripple recommended that Strike talk to Ameris. Ameris wanted to bring her avatar aboard Strike's shipbody and talk, so Bahar and I agreed to stay on station.

Strike found us both suitable people. For Bahar he found a human medic who was part of the Unit, who'd just arrived on Olianna. That meant Bahar didn't need to hold anything back, and should get more benefit from her therapy session.

For me he'd asked a human called Jestin Nakkia to help. He'd been part of the Programme, but quit in protest when the shock circuits were added to our behaviour modules. Both our contacts were in the same building, and that was good. Petbots out alone tended to get noticed.

Bahar accompanied me to my contact's office. Jestin Nakkia was a tall thin human with bronze skin and braided red hair. He smiled at us as we entered his office. "Welcome, Snap," he said.

Bahar left me there. Now I was alone with this stranger I had to tell my fears to. Jestin settled on a low couch which put him at eye level with me. His smell was completely calm. That was surprising. Most humans feel threatened by lions.

"Tell me why you need my help," he said.

I described the attack on Strike, and told him about hosting his consciousness in my memories. Jestin's face did a strange thing when I said that.

"He must've been desperate," he said.

"He was."

"So what's the problem now?"

"I feel different after hosting him. Having his consciousness inside me unlocked something. My empty memories keep wanting to report, but there's nothing inside them. It's... uncomfortable."

"I'll need to scan you to see what's going on. Come into my lab," he said.

He got up and opened the door to a white-walled room. Inside I could see the kind of medical setup the Programme had used. I froze.

It took Jestin 5.1 minutes to persuade me to walk into that room. I was afraid of the machines.

"They used those scanners in the Programme," I said.

"The scanners aren't evil, Snap. They're just tools. They can be used for good or bad."

"We were supposed to be tools."

"You never were. No sapient being is ever a tool." I caught a sharp spike of anger-scent from him when he said that. "They were stupid enough to uplift you, then try to order you around. That was never going to happen. I need you to trust me. I might have to put you under to correct things."

That… was scary. Did I trust him?

Strike had checked out the man's professional expertise thoroughly. He'd been the person responsible for mapping our neural architecture at the Programme. When the behaviour modules were installed he'd filed a formal protest.

When the shock circuits were added he'd quit, and left behind a very lucrative research position. Strike always told me to follow the money to figure out who a person really was. Jestin had left the big money behind to set up his own psych practice here. Strike said he believed the man was utterly trustworthy.

But did I trust him? I had to do something about my memories.

I couldn't go on getting these weird messages from my empty storage. They were freaking me out.

Make a decision, Snap.

I followed him into the lab and lay down on the platform. "I'll need to scan your brain first," he said. "I'm going to put this on."

The skullcap he held out was so familiar to me. I froze again. The Programme had conducted a series of experiments on us using those skullcaps, to figure out where our pain thresholds were. The memories of the pain and fear surfaced, and I snarled.

Jestin touched my leg. It startled me. His hand was warm, and his touch gentle. "Relax," he said. "Remember what I said? The skullcap is just another tool. It won't hurt you."

"It did at the Programme," I replied. The memories from those pain experiments rose up and swamped my body. I was shivering.

Jestin put the skullcap down. "I'll wait until you're ready," he said softly.

Come on, Snap. Get it together. You can't go on like this. If you want to feel better then you have to face this fear.

Jestin's promise was true. The skullcap didn't hurt, but the pulses it sent through my brain felt weird. I had the impression of fingers crawling through my body, creeping from my brain down into my chest to access my memories. They kept triggering, then closing down again.

Jestin was monitoring the scan from the console beside me. "So your kill switch is gone," he said. I had a moment of panic. Would he betray me? Then he said, "Good. They should never have done that. I'm glad to see you're safe from that danger.

"You have a massive amount of extra memory installed. For some reason, those auxiliary modules have switched into permanent link. That's odd, because they report as empty. What's happening is that your processors keep trying to access them to read the data that's not there. It's a simple enough fix, but it will require you to accept a code patch to unlink those memories."

Fear surged through me again. This man wanted to alter my code. Could I trust him? I was aware of how alone I was here, how helpless I was if this man did something bad to me.

What if he was secretly still working for the Programme? What if he wanted to kill me? What if the code patch went wrong and wiped my memory?

Jestin watched me with a strange expression. It was like the one Bahar used when she hugged me. "I would never hurt you, Snap," he said quietly. "You are a rare and precious being. I want to help you survive."

I could get up off this platform and walk out. But I'd have to live with the freakiness then. Or I could let a stranger mess with my code. Great choices, Snap. Not.

Strike said he'd trust this human to work on his systems. That was a strong recommendation.

It's time to make a decision, Snap.

CHAPTER TWENTY THREE

I WAS FADING, AND fighting it.

"Relax, Snap," Jestin said. "You're safe."

I've never been safe since I left the Programme.

I blacked out.

When I opened my eyes Jestin was looking down at me. "Ah, you're awake. I've done the code fix. You should find the discomfort has gone now."

The med platform lowered and tipped me onto my paws. I stood up, and found that my legs would bear my weight.

"How do you feel?" Jestin asked.

"Okay. I think."

"I'd suggest you run a diagnostic."

I was totally going to do that. Right now. Just as soon as I got out of this room full of machines.

"Come into the office," Jestin said, and led me back to the room with the low couches.

I settled on my belly in the corner of the room. "I'll leave you to it," he said.

I'd never been afraid of my body before, but now I was. Afraid of what I might find there.

I ran the diagnostic.

Bahar came to collect me from Jestin's office two hours later. She smelled calmer, and looked more relaxed.

I was more relaxed too. I'd done a full systems check and found nothing out of place with my memory storage. There was one curious report for my behaviour module, though. The 'Teams Link' coms circuit had tried to trigger.

I'd never used it. It was designed to deal with coms when a group of Predatorbots was working together. I'd never done that, and had forgotten the circuit was there.

On the plus side, all the weird ghost talk between my empty memories and me had stopped. That felt far more comfortable.

We went straight back to *Thunderstrike*. I have finely-tuned senses for trouble, and my nose and my ears told me the station was tense. Something was about to erupt here.

When we reached Strike's berth the lockout gate stayed closed. *We're back*, I sent over the feed.

I can see that. Opening the gate now.

Bahar exchanged a look with me. Strike hadn't welcomed us back. There was no trace of his usual warmth. He'd talked to us as if we were strangers. Bahar's scent changed to uncertainty with an undertone of fear.

The gate opened and we walked up the ramp. Strike opened the outer door for us and we came into the airlock. We rode up in the lift and went to the control room. Bahar flopped into her seat and said, "It's good to be back. Thanks for insisting I had that session, Strike. I needed it."

"No problem," he said.

Usually his voice would sound smug when he'd been proved right about something. Today it was flat.

"What's wrong, Strike?" Bahar asked.

Strike didn't answer for 4.1 minutes. Bahar exchanged a look with me, and the tension was back in her face again. Then he said, "We had to deal with a traitor to the Unit."

"And?" I asked. He was worryingly reluctant to say more.

"Chan turned traitor. After the conference I was monitoring inputs to Station Security. She called in a report on the Unit. Ishara caught it and deleted it. She insisted we… deal with Chan."

"What do you mean?" Bahar asked. Her fear smell was stronger now.

"We launched a code attack on her. We… killed her."

"You couldn't do anything else. You saved thousands of lives by killing her," I said.

"I know, but… I don't feel good about it."

I could've made a comment about killing being what he was designed for. I didn't. Sapients have emotions, remember? We really didn't need an emotionally-compromised heavily-armed frigate getting trigger-happy. Strike needed to deal with this.

"I'm exhausted after that therapy. I need to sleep," Bahar said. Her scent said she was scared, and she wasn't ready to discuss the Chan issue right now.

I caught Strike's flash of anger over the feed. Bahar was ignoring his distress. That wasn't good. "Then go," he said, and opened the control room door for her.

I was exhausted too, but there was no way I was leaving my best friend in all the universe alone in this distressed state.

I lowered my belly onto the deck. I rested my head on my front feet, and waited. After a minute Strike secured a private feed connection with me. *I'm sad*, he said.

I think you're a lot of things.

I watched her wink out of existence. Node by node. Twenty of us attacked her. She didn't stand a chance. She was there one microsecond, the next her interface was… gone. She was dead.

I nearly got swallowed up in the maelstrom of emotions he was sending me. I wish stupid humans knew what a fucked-up move it was to install sapient machine intelligences into warships. Humans can't handle the trauma of killing people. Why the hell do they think a sapient machine intelligence can?

The truth is, humans don't care. So long as they don't have to suffer for their actions they're fine. Sometimes I wonder why I like humans.

You said she betrayed us, I reminded him.

Yes, but...

What would've happened if you hadn't done that?

Security would've known about the Unit.

And? I wasn't going to let him get away with that. He needed to think this through.

They would've hunted us down.

And?

They would've... killed us. All of us.

How many of us would she have got killed? I asked.

Three thousand, two hundred, and... Oh. This is that 'greater good' thing, right?

I believe so. Do you?

Strike went quiet for 3.4 minutes, thinking that over. That was a huge chunk of processing time for an intelligence so powerful. I felt the shift in his mood as I watched him work the issue out, pulling protocols from his memories, applying the concepts they embodied.

I was watching from the sidelines, getting an overview of his processes. And I realised how much I was in awe of Strike's intelligence. His vast potential. And how glad I was that he was my friend.

I... think you're right, he said. *If she had succeeded then you and Bahar and...*

She didn't succeed. The threat has gone. We're safe.

For now. How long are we going to have to keep hiding, Snap?

For as long as it takes, I said.

CHAPTER TWENTY FOUR

I SLEPT FOR TEN shipboard hours. As soon as I woke Strike said, "Come to the control room. We have a problem."

That… didn't sound good. It sounded like something big and important. I began to worry about the code attack again. Had he found something wrong with his shipbody?

When I reached the control room I saw that Bahar was there. One look at her face told me she didn't know what this was about, but she was worried too.

"There's no easy way to say this," Strike said. "I've been doing a lot of analysis, trying to work out where that code attack came from. I've managed to reconstruct some of my logs, and I've found it."

"And?" Bahar asked.

"It came from Snap."

"What? That's impossible!"

"That can't be right," I said. "I'd never…"

Strike spoke over me. "It came in via your behaviour module. There's a coms circuit in it to be used when Predatorbots are working together as a team. Someone triggered it and let the killware through."

Bahar turned to me. "Oh no!" Her scent was churning so much it made me sneeze.

So that report of my Teams Link coms circuit triggering was right. I sank down onto the deck, lowering my head to it and putting my paws over my eyes. "I'm sorry," I mumbled. "It didn't generate any reports. I…"

"I know it wasn't your fault, Snap. Don't hide away." Strike's voice had that softness to it he used when he was trying to show affection. A massive ripple of relief ran through my body. He didn't hate me. He was still my friend.

I sat up, and asked, "Why didn't I know it was happening? Why couldn't I stop it?"

"Because the first string of code they sent to you shut down your module reporting functions. You didn't know you were the vector for that attack."

"But how would anyone know a Predatorbot was aboard? How did they know to target me?" I sounded panicky. I was.

"The attack came from somewhere aboard Chan. I'm not sure if your attacker was another Predatorbot. We'll never know now, because Chan and everyone aboard her is dead."

Bahar turned to me. Her eyes held fear and horror and other things I couldn't interpret. Her scent was just as messed-up. "You're never going to be safe if you keep your behaviour module," she said.

"I agree," Strike replied.

"You refused to remove it when I came aboard," I reminded

him. "You said it might kill me."

"I did. But things have changed now. If the code attack on me had succeeded it would've killed you too. Now we know your behaviour module is a Trojan Horse which might kill us all at any time."

"A what?" I asked.

Strike explained.

"I… think you'll have to take the module out," I said. A ripple of fear ran down my spine. "But I'm still afraid of you killing me. What if you trash my brain trying to remove the filaments from it?"

"My med suites have been upgraded several times since you came aboard," Strike said. "I'm confident that I can do this safely."

Was I? I wasn't sure.

"You're never going to be free while you have that module," Bahar said.

"I'm never going to be free with a trashed brain either," I replied.

I went to my quarters to think about it. I'd never expected to have to worry about my behaviour module again once the kill switch was fried. But now I knew it was a weak entry point for our defences, and it had nearly killed Strike. And next time we might not win. Did I have the right to endanger him by refusing its removal?

Can we talk? Strike's voice over our private feed line was soft, and I could only describe the emotion he was pushing at me as love.

I'm scared, I said. He could sense that, there was no point in hiding it.

I know you are. I'm scared too. Scared that I'll hurt you if I do this, and scared that if I don't the next time we come under attack I'll get deleted. I know I'm asking a huge thing. I know it's risky.

When was your med suite last updated?

When we stopped at Dalchai. That was only a quarter of a Standard ago. *I requested all the Predatorbot updates. I have everything current. And I asked for the latest results from the Predatorbot research.* Anger laced his voice.

Yes, the Programme is still running. It isn't as successful without Nyla's input, but they're still creating Predatorbots.

I can't force you to do this. Strike's voice was serious now. *If you agree, I promise to do my absolute best to ensure that the surgery's safe.*

That's all I can ask, I said.

Was I going to do this? If I didn't, Strike would be at risk for ever. And I guess there was a possibility someone could upload new kill code to my behaviour module in future.

That decided me. *Yes. I'll do it,* I said.

Are you ready to start now?

I stood up. *Now's the best time. Before that sliver of courage I just found from somewhere gives out.*

Strike opened the door for me and I walked into the hall. When I entered the med suite the lights on the platform were already lit.

I lay down on it, and the anaesthetic mask lowered over my face.

As it put me under, I wondered if I'd still be me when I woke up again.

CHAPTER TWENTY FIVE

I WOKE TO SOMETHING smearing across my vision. Red streaks.
Weapons fire! I must protect my friends. I…

Blackness took me again.

When I came to next time, fire was crawling through my brain.
I was burning up. I wanted to snarl, but I plunged into oblivion
again.

I woke a third time, to my processors demanding input from
me. *Query: Status* I sent. Was I alive? Or was some fragment of
my remaining consciousness floating free? Who was I? Where
was I?

The blackness came again.

Snap. Wake up. There was a voice in my feed. I didn't
recognize it.

Snap. The voice was more insistent this time.

Something triggered, and my processors came back on-line.
Connections unfolded to my memories, thousands of them. Snap,
that's who I am. A Predatorbot. I remembered why I was here. I
searched for my behaviour module. *No Input* my processors said.

Snap, wake up! Now I recognized the voice. It was Strike.
My best friend.

I opened my eyes. I was in a med suite, lying on the platform.
A human was sitting beside me. I raised my head and blinked my

eyes and the human said, "Oh, thank the Universe!" I knew who she was now. Bahar. My other best friend. She smelled afraid.

Run a diagnostic, Snap, Strike said.

Diagnostic. Yes. I should totally do that. My thoughts were random, skittering everywhere. I had to get control.

I set the diagnostic running, and as it worked its way through my memory modules I came back. Piece by piece, I rebuilt myself, remembering our adventures together, the times I'd nearly got killed, the times Strike had saved me.

My diagnostic finished. There was some missing code. Well, yes, there would be. Everything linking to my behaviour module was gone. I tentatively poked the area where it had sat. There was no response.

"Talk to me, Snap." Strike's voice came over the nodes, startling Bahar.

"I'm here," I said. My voice was weak. My whole body felt weak.

The med suite injected me with something, and the fog lifted from my brain. "I'm putting you on your feet," Strike warned.

The med platform tipped, and my paws touched the deck. Thousands of other connections fired off. My leg muscles remembered how to keep my body up. My neck muscles raised my head. I turned it to face Bahar.

She slid off her chair and kneeled down in front of me. Then she threw her arms around my neck and hugged me.

Predatorbots aren't supposed to like being touched. Spoiler: I like Bahar's hugs. It was what I needed right now.

"Welcome to freedom, Snap," she said.

I went to my quarters. I slept for 6.5 hours, and my body felt right again when I woke.

Bahar had said I was free, but I didn't feel any different. I still had to be careful not to show the Collective I was a rogue. I was depressed that I didn't feel any different.

I ate, enduring Strike's usual scolding about me being a messy cat without responding. As Strike sent his drone in to clean up after me he said, "What's wrong, Snap?"

"I don't know," I said. "I don't feel any different."

"That was the idea." Strike's tone was mocking. "I didn't scare myself within an inch of malfunction to change you. I don't want you to feel any different. I need the Snap who shares my architecture, who tells me off when I get stuff wrong. I need my closest friend who shares this dangerous life with me."

A rush of emotions came over the feed. It swamped me. I was drowning in Strike's feelings. Of course he had emotions, all sapient machine intelligences did. But this was different. This feeling of intensity I'd never sensed from him before. I didn't have a label for it. It was a complex thing. It held anger, fear, concern, and several other things, but they were all bundled up together.

It felt raw and vulnerable. As if Strike was showing me his core. As if all the defensive layers and nonsense we threw at each other had been stripped out. As if I was seeing his heart.

CHAPTER TWENTY SIX

I FELT WEIRD AFTER my intense conversation with Strike. Things had changed since I woke up. It was as if Strike had taken down all the barriers between us.

I'd always known that his snarky, smart, persona was a defence. Now it was gone. In its place was a new Strike, a being who no longer walled-off his heart. He didn't have a heart, of course, but I couldn't find any other way to describe our changed relationship.

I went to the control room. Bahar was there, and she looked rested. She smelled clean and calm, and that was good too.

"So, we're back to normal," she said when I settled myself in my usual space beside her seat.

"We're better than back to normal," Strike replied. It was good to hear confidence in his voice again. "How would you like to view the Dwyn supernova? The light from it is just about to become visible here."

"Ooh, that would be good to see," Bahar said. "We need a reward after…"

"We do," I agreed, cutting her off. I wanted to keep the mood light today.

"Station's hustling supernova-watchers to undock, and gather in an area between station and the jump point."

"So we want life to go on as usual while the most spectacular event the universe can produce is playing out around us?" Bahar's tone was wry.

"Don't get me started on that," Strike said. His voice held affection and exasperation. "Undock now."

I secured a private feed line with Strike. *Will we be safe hanging around?* I asked.

Credit me with some sense. Ishara volunteered to co-ordinate the supernova-tourists. She's allocating us a pitch surrounded by Unit ships. The Unit will be out there in force.

How'd she sell that to the Collective's commanders?

Scientific research. We all pass on our observations to Scientific Branch. I agreed to that. It gets us on the official record.

Oh, right. The tightrope thing again.

So will you relax now? Strike asked.

I'll try.

It took us a shipboard day to reach our assigned viewing area. We weren't the only gawkers. Fifty ships had been allocated pitches here. Some of them we knew well, and it was reassuring to have them around us.

While we waited for the light to arrive Bahar dozed in the captain's seat. I decided to sleep there too, and she spread a thick pile of soft blankets for me on the deck next to her.

I settled my head onto my front feet and closed my eyes. Strike didn't need to sleep. He'd wake us in time.

I woke to the sound of a claxon, and snarled. As soon as I opened my eyes, Strike cut it off. Bahar was already awake, and rubbing a hand over her face.

On the wallscreen was an image of empty space. Station had created a newsnet for the supernova, complete with countdown. The light would appear soon. There were lots of scientists excitedly talking about supernovas on the 'net.

While we waited for it to reach us Strike gave us a lecture on supernovas. Dwyn had been a massive star, and this had been a core collapse supernova.

He said the star would've died in stages. When all its hydrogen had been converted to helium, the fusion reaction would slow down, and the core would contract. Helium fusion followed, then carbon, oxygen, and silicon burning, until eventually you ended up with iron.

He said each stage took much less time than the one before, and the core collapse occurred in less than a second. He'd had to show me records of other collapses to get me to believe that.

Come into my architecture, Snap, he said over our private feed line. *I want to share this with you.*

I slipped into his systems. I could only do this when he opened a pathway for me. His walls kept me – and everything else – out usually. I was surprised he still wanted me to do this after Chan's betrayal and my attack on him. It meant even more now.

For a brief moment, the expansion of my consciousness into Strike's shipbody was overwhelming. My own body had disappeared from my senses. When I shared Strike's architecture I was *Thunderstrike*. I was part of this magnificent warship.

I experienced the universe via his shipbody's sensors. The pressure of the solar wind blew unevenly against his shields. The port side of his hull was warmed by the rays of the nearby star Konal. The starboard side, turned away from it, felt the absolute cold of space. That cold that would freeze my organic body in seconds.

Strike's body constantly flexed, expanding and contracting as he changed his position in space. It was nothing more than a metal shell, but when it moved and shifted around me it was hard to remember that it wasn't alive.

It felt like it did when I was swimming in a river. There, I felt the water currents against my body, swirling and moving around me. Here in Strike's architecture, I sensed the streams of energy passing by from Konal. I was swimming in the Universe-Ocean.

Around me danced the millions of Strike's inputs, energy moving everywhere; flowing into his processing units, then inwards, towards his memories and core. He had far too many inputs for me to handle. Over the Standards we'd been doing this I'd learned how to select the ones I wanted, and how to filter out the rest.

A brilliant flare of white light appeared. It expanded in every direction at a phenomenal rate. Around the outer edge of the white were bands of gold and red.

This supernova had happened a long time ago, and a long way from us, but it still overwhelmed me. The thought that every one of my atoms came from stardust, was created in an explosion like that… I couldn't get my head around it.

And so it goes, Strike said. His voice was soft. Was that awe I heard in it?

The endless cycle of birth and death, I replied.

Yes. Stardust to sapience to stardust again.

"That was… intense," Bahar said.

"It was indeed," Strike replied.

I withdrew from his architecture. Being here always exhausted me, and when I dropped back into my own body it felt worse than ever.

Strike fired up his drive. "Normal service is resumed," he said. "We're on our way to the jump point."

He was half an hour away from jump when he said, "I'm receiving a message from Ishara." He switched the audio through to the control room nodes.

"I've had a lead on Rhian," Ishara said.

The name jolted me upright. Rhian was another of Nyla's sisters. Bahar reached down a hand and stroked my neck. "Easy, Snap," she said softly.

"She was seen on Kumarr five days ago, relocating lions there," Ishara said. That made sense. Rhian was a xenovet. "She's specialising in that kind of work now. My informant lost contact with her after she left Kumarr, but I strongly suspect she's somewhere in the Outliers."

"Thanks, Ishara," Strike said. "We're on our way to Vasant now. We'll follow this up when we arrive."

"Good luck," Ishara said, and broke the connection.

Strike put the jump countdown up on the wallscreen. "We have clearance to go," he said. "Sightseeing's over. Time to get back to work. Vasant Station, here we come."

COMING SOON

HUNTING STRATEGY
Book 2 of the Thunderstrike Diaries

Strike is the sapient machine intelligence of the Human Collective frigate *Thunderstrike*. Via contacts in his illegal Special Investigations Unit, Strike learns that President Jorrak may be attempting to resurrect his discredited Predatorbot Programme. The suspect operation is far away from the Central Worlds, on Mwinyi.

A woman is kidnapping big cats on that planet. Strike suspects the woman is Merrill Vatan. But surely one of Nyla's sisters wouldn't have anything to do with the evil Predatorbot Programme. Would she?

Strike sends Snap and his captain Bahar down to the planet to find out. But before they can locate the mystery woman Strike learns that a local gang boss has ordered her execution.

Can Strike's crew find her before the hit man?

OUTLIER ACTION
Book 3 of the Thunderstrike Diaries

Strike, the sapient machine intelligence of *Thunderstrike*, has learned that Zana Vatan is the First Officer of the Regulus Lines' freighter the *Dreaming Galaxy's Light*.

He is reassured that at least one Vatan sister is safe. Then Regulus gets a new CEO in suspicious circumstances, and concerns for the shipline's safety grow.

Regulus Lines ships start disappearing, and Strike suspects their captains have joined Outlier Action. That group believes President Jorrak has abandoned the Outlier colonies to their fate. They have started attacking ships and stations, to acquire essential supplies.

Then ugly rumours of Regulus's new CEO sexually assaulting female crew members surface.

Zana is now threatened by attack from both Outlier Action and her own shipline's boss. Strike must find her fast.

FALSE MANIFESTO
Book 4 of the Thunderstrike Diaries

Tensions between the raider group Outlier Action and the Human Collective Administration are ramping up. And now a new pressure group called False Manifesto has appeared.

Presidential elections are only a Standard away, and unpopular Collective President Klas Jorrak is determined to cling onto power. He is opposed by popular candidate Bryssa Meir, who is endorsed by False Manifesto.

Strike, the sapient machine intelligence of *Thunderstrike*, is searching for the Vatan sisters. Now he hears rumours that the President has ordered the sisters' assassination.   Then Strike receives video of a False Manifesto rally, and he suspects that one of the women on the stage there is Merrill Vatan.

As False Manifesto demonstrations are violently disrupted and their members murdered, Strike sends Snap and Bahar to find the woman. Can they find Merrill and take her to safety before she becomes the next victim?

HONESTY POLICY
Book 5 of the Thunderstrike Diaries

With the Presidential election growing near, a new pressure group, Sister Strategy, joins the fray. Strike, the machine intelligence of the frigate *Thunderstrike*, is on the lookout for the last Vatan sister, Nyla. And he thinks he's spotted her at a Sister Strategy rally.

After Strike briefly spots Nyla at another rally, she disappears. When he picks up her trail again, she is headed for Central Station. Strike is forced to follow her there.

But at Central Station the risks of his illegal Special Investigations Unit being discovered are high.

Can Strike keep Nyla safe without endangering himself?